THE WHITE FLOWER

Charlotte Beeston

D1806611

LesFugitives
London

This first English-language edition published
by Les Fugitives editions in the United Kingdom in November 2024 •
• Les Fugitives Ltd, 91 Cholmley Gardens, Fortune Green Road, London NW6 1UN •
• www.lesfugitives.com • Cover illustration from a photograph by Dominic Lee,
courtesy of the artist • Cover design by Sarah Schulte and Dominic Lee •
• Text design by Juliette Lépineau • All rights reserved •
• No part of this publication may be reproduced, stored in a retrieval
system or transmitted in any form or by any means, electronic,
mechanical, photocopying, recording or otherwise, without
prior permission in writing from Les Fugitives editions •
• A CIP catalogue record for this book is available from the British Library •
• The rights of Charlotte Beeston to be identified as author of this
work have been identified in accordance with Section 77 of the
Copyright, Designs and Patents Act 1988 • Printed in England by
CMP, Poole, Dorset • ISBN: 978-1-7397783-8-5 •

'Charlotte Beeston's gorgeous debut novel, *The White Flower*, is a wonderfully intelligent and sensitively handled portrait of grief, how it leaves us obsessively circling the same moments, scenes and images. Literary in the best sense (language matters), the novel is full of incidental pleasures and deserves to be widely read.'
– **Andrew Miller**, author of *The Slowworm's Song*

'An ode to grief, Charlotte Beeston's *The White Flower* renders the physicality of loss and yearning in prose so very exquisite.'
– **Cauvery Madhavan**, author of *The Tainted* and *The Inheritance*

'This beautifully written narrative alternates between Stella's contemporary story set in London and Julia's Edwardian one, set in East Devon and London. Stella and Julia's individual meditations on their deep losses combine to form an emotionally intelligent, thought-provoking portrait of grief and the mother-daughter bond. It's raw and compelling and brilliant on letting life in and finding slivers of hope in the darkest situations. It stayed with me long after I finished it.'
– **Sara Lawrence**, *Daily Mail*

the quick brown fox ~

THE WHITE FLOWER

For my mother

... if I did not *know*, at least I *felt* ...

Charlotte Brontë, *Villette*

To the north of the village, there is rainforest. Foliage is dense, rich, green. Trees have snow-white barks, gnarled and blistered with age. Tread lightly, reverently, for this place is holy. Ruined temples with carved stones hold the ashes of unremembered kings and queens. In the heart of the forest stands the holy tree. A cutting imported from far away, it now rises, magnificent. The oldest living tree planted by a human; it is said to be a seedling of the Bodhi tree of enlightenment. Its heart-shaped leaves are prized.

At dusk, bells summon the pious to worship. They arrive silently with baskets of floral offerings: white jasmine, gardenia, champak. The air is heavy with the sweetness of temple flowers laid at the tree's altar as marks of love and gratitude. Symbols, too, of both the transience of earthly joy and the permanence of the eternal. For while their white sweetness will fade by nightfall, having possessed beauty, these flowers share in the eternal and can never vanish in decay.

Stella

Deep winter. November has withdrawn its winds and fogs to settle on distant lands. The sky is clear, crystalline. The river glitters.

A cold night. Stars are hidden, always hidden, for this is London. Oblongs of light from offices and houses fall among bare trees. She stares blankly from one of these windows, unsure if she has heard something, but the road outside is empty, still, with only the faint murmur of an overground train.

After a while, she goes back to bed. There are used napkins on her bedside table, a wineglass with dark remnants. She feels crumbs in the sheets as she turns onto her front and lifts her long hair from her back. The silence seems to punish her.

For a long time, she tries to summon sleep, falling eventually into a thin, fretful slumber. Her mind fills with distorted memories of the day. A dim living room. Framed paintings covering the walls. Oil brushstrokes in yellows, browns, greens and blue. A vast collection of hardback books piled haphazardly on shelves. The room shifts in her mind, tangles with memories of another home. A similar crowd of colours and textures, but there is her grandmother's sideboard, the collection of blue Persian plates, delicately glazed. She stops breathing for a moment, lets out a small whimper, then turns on her side. Hours pass until the sounds of early traffic come through the window: the first bus of the day, the shriek of an ambulance. She listens vaguely to the noises outside, layers of sleep falling away. After a while, she sits up, looks drowsily around her, then pulls on a long-sleeved, rumpled black dress from the floor, washes and leaves her apartment.

The old lift in her building rises slowly, slower still if a neighbour is waiting beside her, and when it arrives, she steps in quickly, relieved to be alone. As the lift descends, she looks at herself in the mirror. Her skin appears sallow and dehydrated, or perhaps it is only distorted in the artificial light?

Outside, the sun is unclouded, pale gold, and the pavements are still wet with the damp of early morning. Only now can she relax, let out a deep sigh and think about the day ahead. Another meeting in his flat off Earl's Court Road. He advised regular appointments at the beginning and she has complied so far, lacking the will to protest.

She enjoys the walk from the Underground, the quieter, residential streets, takes her time before turning into a narrow alleyway. Several ailing potted plants group together on the ground opposite his front door, their leaves reaching out for light. Her knock is tentative, quiet.

As she waits, she glances back along the path, angles her face towards the low sun, enjoying its mellow warmth on her skin. Try to find the beauty of the now, he has urged, little pockets of happiness. This will help with the dwelling on the past, the worrying about the future. But she never allows herself to think of the future. Not because she doesn't believe in it, for she knows life will go on. It is simply that the future offers more of the same, and more of the same is unbearable.

She hears a rustling within, the rasp of a bolt and he appears, soft navy scarf tied close to his chin, dark curly hair. He shuts the door behind her quickly, as if to shut out the light, then leads her into the living room. It is dark after being outside, though not unwelcoming. A candle casts golden semi-circles across the table. In the centre, a jug with flowers. An empty sheet of paper. She has read some of what he has written about her. He showed her a passage last time, but she said nothing.

Before sitting down, she allows herself a moment to look at his paintings. There is a portrait she hasn't noticed before. An angular, tilting head with hand cupped to ear, in pink-brown tones, the brushstrokes thick. It reminds her of an early self-portrait by Lucien Freud, yet the subject is undoubtedly the man seated opposite. He follows her gaze and glances over his shoulder.

From one of my patients, he says, picking up his pen. So, how are you feeling today?

She looks away, not knowing how to answer. The truth is she never knows. She is unpractised in deciphering her emotions, these untethered and unfathomable sensations, knows only that they're capable of overwhelming her.

I'm OK.

That's not a feeling.

Sorry. I don't know. I should write them down.

You should be feeling them. He smiles gently, encouragingly. Did anything come up after our last session? Have you thought any more about the accident?

She has thought about it. The foot caught in the cord on the kitchen counter. Boiling water from the kettle. Searing pain. The fabric of her school dress welded to her skin.

I don't think I did it on purpose, she says. Her words make them both shift slightly. As he takes her back through the incident – her mother's face, the journey to the hospital, the extended stay at the burns unit – she wants only to be outside in daylight. She gazes at his blue and white striped shirt. When she does speak, her voice is so dry she has to swallow.

Rather than going home afterwards, she heads for Shoreditch High Street, emerging from the Underground near Spitalfields Market and cutting across onto

Commercial Street. She needs to be near flowers, the comforting green of vegetation, and heads towards a familiar row of russet-coloured shrubs and winter berries. Soon she is breathing in a damp, earthy smell. The door to the flower shop is open and a woman is inside, stripping leaves from stems, her long auburn hair swept off her face. She makes Stella feel welcome, encourages her to talk while arranging a bunch of flowers.

A golden light. She is pressed tight against warm, sweet-smelling skin, coconut scented. Tall, feathery shapes sway nearby. The rasp of a spade slicing through soil.

To feel that presence again. To be near it. And so Stella idles among flowers and plants and all things that grow, even in the middle of the city. She searches out the capital's hidden gardens, small patches of wilderness disowned by the local council or forgotten by developers. There is one at the end of Long Lane, another behind the Barbican.

Later, in a coffee shop, when someone approaches, she realises she is crying. Grey suit, crisp blue shirt, big smile. He thrusts a slice of cake at her.

I thought it might cheer you up. You looked upset.

Before she can respond, he is gone, away into the road with the other office workers. His unexpected kindness takes her by surprise. She is never looking for it. Out of the shop now, she is on her way home, striding fast. Her mind is agitated and restless. She realises that she wants her mother to run to her, with the horror of seeing her scalded body, to wrap her in a damp sheet, and to echo what Stella is already feeling, that she has never needed her more.

Julia

East Devon, July 1910 – I need to write this down.
To make sense of it. For months have passed and
I have travelled and yet, still you are with me. How
to be free from this agony? But not from you, never
free from you. I am looking up at a cloudless sky, extraordinarily blue. A white blaze of sun. From where
I stand, on the headland, the cliffs are not far from
my feet. Shall I hurl myself to be closer to you, my
beloved? You for whom I've shed all my tears?

Your room is untouched. Your bed in polished
mahogany wood. The dressing table with a
three-fold mirror, the tray of pins and decorative
combs you used in your long hair. Your photograph
albums, your Japanese prints on the wall. Lying in
bed, you would ask for your sketches, your eyes
looking for one in particular. The vast fig tree.
I would place it on the pillow beside you, stroke your
forehead as you stared at it. It brought you more
comfort than your own mother, or so it seemed.

At your funeral, there was a woman I didn't
recognise, who did not come to the reception
afterwards. She placed a small bunch of lilies beside

your coffin with a white card attached. 'Deepest sympathy, all my love, Grace'.

I looked at your wooden coffin as it was lowered into the earth and stared down into the grave. There you lay, my daughter, my Helena. There were things about you I would never understand, but no part of you I could live without.

I was afraid, my darling, afraid that I would faint, but I had to look. I had to feel, the last chance that was left to me.

Stella

She wakes early, already anxious. The sky is deep mauve. The river is luminous, rushing in silver-blue peaks. A large branch is being carried away by the tide, and she watches it dip under, then re-emerge several times until it disappears from view. By nine o'clock, the sky has darkened and the river is dull grey. Fleets of Thames Clippers take commuters to work. A police boat passes back and forth. The racing and swirling water, the bustle of traffic upon it, are welcome distractions, for in these quiet moments alone, she is uneasy, unable to settle. She feels an increasing restlessness, a sense of having done something wrong. Of being wrong.

It reminds her, all those years ago, when her father would come home from work and immediately a dark mood seeped through the house. She couldn't bear to be around it, would go upstairs and play alone in her bedroom, all the while anticipating footsteps on the landing, the creak of the corner step. She would pause, hold her breath, remain silent. Sometimes, her father would listen on the other side of the door. At other times, he would knock, then immediately enter and scan the room with a fierce expression on his face. The constant surveillance of her childhood. The worry that something she did might disappoint and she would be punished. A noise she made, a careless act or simply behaviour that irritated, would be wrong. When she heard her father's retreating steps, she would tip-toe over to the window and look out. At the overgrown fields, to the trees beyond, the distant clouds.

And although she is no longer in that bedroom, she still feels the same unease when someone presses the button for the communal lift, the unbelievably slow lift, and waits on the other side of her door. In that pause, always the possibility of rebuke.

Eleven in the morning, the penetrating cold of winter in the air. She leaves her apartment, goes into one of the cafés nearby, and orders a coffee. She doesn't want coffee, but cannot spend a moment longer in her flat. As she sits down, she catches sight of her face in the mirror opposite, at the deepening hollows under her eyes. Thirty-one soon. She will never be any younger, yet she wishes she could start her life again.

A couple sit at a table overlooking the river. They are reading from menus. The woman seems very self-assured, tapping a crimson fingernail as she decides what to order. The man keeps looking at her. Perhaps that is why Stella is here, in the hope of absorbing their composure. Perhaps it is all a performance.

She wonders if she sees her therapist's real self or whether it is also an act. She thinks of their session yesterday. He was alive with work, his hair falling in his face as he explained what they were doing. He'd sat very close to her and tapped softly on the back of her hands, first the right then the left, back and forth, back and forth. Then at the end, there was a test, or it had felt like a test. To assimilate the memories, to say precisely what came into her mind.

Were her reflections honest? Did they come from a need to please or, at least, not disappoint him? He was apparently satisfied because after a while she heard him lean back in his chair, ask her to think of her calm place. This was the signal to stop remembering, to return to the present.

In their first session, she had chosen a deserted beach. Purple-pink pebbles stretching for miles. Water flowing in, flowing out. Hot sun burnishing her shoulders, her face. And as she'd thought of it, her breathing had steadied and fallen into an even rhythm. In that moment, she felt not so much a physical calm, but something even deeper, the throb of her heart, of life itself. When she opened her eyes, he was looking at her earrings. She had worn them on purpose. Painterly in style, with blue swirls across a white background, like clouds in the sky or a surging sea.

Afterwards, she caught the bus that took her home, past rows of white mansion blocks and redbrick houses with tall windows. She was conscious of her facial expressions, her body on the seat. Nothing she did felt natural, as though she'd changed into somebody else.

She found herself getting off at an earlier stop, going into the National Gallery. Drifting through its long salons, past Velázquez and Canaletto, she reached the Impressionists. Everything was washed in muted light and silence. After some time, she followed a young couple outside and into one of the squares behind the gallery. They strolled into a gated garden in the centre, with glossy green leaves, manicured lawns and newly painted benches. One or two windows in the surrounding houses were illuminated, showing glimpses of carefully arranged furniture. Everything looked new and clean. She wanted to take the newness with her.

And now she is lingering in a café amid the low, murmuring talk of other people, as the light slowly shifts along the river. Later in the day, she will return home, her fingers white and numb from walking outside, her footsteps loud on the frosty pavements. She will let herself into her apartment and immediately feel its emptiness. The furniture standing silent, the kitchen cold and unused. She will turn on all the lights, determined to assert her presence on it.

Julia

The water is very calm today and so clear I can see the stones at the bottom. My eyes follow the line of cliffs running out to sea, red sandstone blending with white chalk, to the hazy pink bulks in the distance. I have come here, beside the tall grasses, to write my diary, and yet I keep thinking of your sister. I mustn't neglect her or take for granted those who are still alive. I cannot spend the rest of my life trying to get back to you.

Louisa is doing her best to care for me, preparing my meals and suggesting how we might spend our days, but it is hard to show any enthusiasm. You know how much I used to enjoy visiting her, every summer, for seven, no, eight years now. But this year is different. Everything is different.

Edward, the gardener, collected me from the railway station by horse and cart, and I imagined you were there as we jolted out onto the coastal road, passing stone cottages with thatched roofs and little gardens bright with sea-pinks and mar-guerites, before emerging into open countryside. The road took us through ploughed fields and hedgerows blossoming with hawthorn, and then dropped down a small hill. The horse settled into a slow jog trot until we turned the corner and suddenly there was the coast.

You loved the sea. The water was alive, you said, it told you things. Agitated waves, tipped with white foam, warned of rising winds. Still blue water, glistening like silk, promised a calm day, and when the water ran red, enfolding ruddy-coloured soil in its waves, you thought something was bleeding beneath its surface. It is ever-present, the sea, visible from every window in Louisa's house. Living with it every day makes me feel closer to you.

Yesterday Louisa and I walked the headland. A steep climb in places, I had to lean far over, head bowed, ankles tightening with each step. Puffing our way to the top, we rested for a moment, then continued along a dipping path through woodland until we reached the cliff edge. There was the sea: wrinkled and blue and endless. I had a sudden urge to throw myself towards it, past the slipping, crumbling land covered in ferns and tall yellow flowers. These impulses take me by surprise. I have them frequently: on the edge of the cliff, the balcony of my bedroom. I have never felt such destructive urges

before. Has this violence been within me all along?
Am I partly responsible for what happened to you?
Forgive me. I can't allow myself to think that.
Diana is so very different from you. She is less
intense, has less fight, although sometimes a calm
surface conceals powerful emotions. Your moods
were always visible and at times explosive, as if
needing release. Is that fair, my darling? I feared for
how you felt and the choices you made because
I only knew some of it. Your letters from Ceylon
began to make no sense and they troubled me
deeply. Allow the mind to wander and it will take
you to far darker places than reality often bears out.
I could never make your father understand.
He is not the easiest of men. I know that. He can
be disinterested, even reproachful at times, but I
don't think there was anything about his behaviour
that caused conflict in your childhood or left a
lasting impression on you. He showed such devotion
when you and Diana were babies. He couldn't
leave you alone! Promising me he wouldn't lift you
from your cots while you slept, and yet, after I'd
left the room, doing just that. But perhaps as you
grew older, my darling, some sort of lack in your
relationship developed.

On my first evening here, I stood in my petticoat washing myself, then slipped on my evening dress in front of the looking glass. I fastened your heart-shaped pendant around my neck and leaned in to closer examine my reflection. I am getting old, my love. There are wrinkles across my forehead, shadows and creases where my skin was once firm. These signs of ageing no longer disturb me. What does any of it matter when you are not here?

As I lie on the headland, the sky opens wide in front of me, pure blue without a single cloud. Everything is still. I feel your presence fasten around me as if you were here, as if you were in the birdsong, the earth, the scent of pine trees, the sound of the sea. A moment of absolute peace tips over me before all that I have lost rushes back in.

Stella

She has begun to feel a gentle ache below her clavicle, close to where she imagines her heart to be. On some days, it's more pronounced than others. Softer than the thudding-pulse of a nightmare, or the fast-patter when anxious, this new sensation fascinates her. Internet diagnoses suggest anything from indigestion to a pulled muscle, but she doesn't believe it is any of these. She dismisses the idea of a smartwatch, for she wants to hear her heart beating inside her. On impulse, she buys a stethoscope from the internet. It arrives the following day, but is delivered to a neighbour and she has to wait two more days before she can unwrap the heavily taped package and hold the steel instrument in her hands.

Lying down on her bed, she parts her white silk shirt and presses the stethoscope's cool silver disc to her heart. The sound is muffled, yet there it is: thud thud thud. Hours pass as she lies on the bed, transfixed by the sound, despite the pinching of the earpieces.

The curtains are open and she watches the moon appear in the sky, full, clear and high above the city. She remembers another pearl-white moon, its light glimpsing across a Formica desk with cards, bunches of flowers in purple gift bags, onto a hospital bed, a white cotton blanket and the outline of her mother's delicate body. Her head is raised from the pillow, tilted towards the window.

It's the moon, Stella whispers, pulling the curtain back as far as it will go.

Her thoughts are punctuated by the steady rhythm of her heart. It pulls her back to the present, to this room, this city, but she can feel herself slipping. She longs for the warmth of her mother's body. It is only sleep that finally separates her from this continual ache, a deep sleep, in spite of the stethoscope at her ears, and when she emerges the following morning, all she can remember of her dreams is a gentle sensation, and a vast expanse that is flat and smooth and white. The stethoscope is on the pillow beside her. She must have removed it in the night.

*

A pale sun rises without heat. The river is silver. She is listening to the houseboats shift and chafe against each other, with a rasping, moaning sound, when a text arrives from Sarah:

I'm coming to Borough Market tomorrow. How about we meet for a coffee? I'd love to see you.

The invitation makes her nervous. She hasn't been in touch with anyone from work since her last day, only calls with HR immediately afterwards, and a thinly compassionate voicemail from her boss. London's sheer mass of inhabitants grants her anonymity: it is rare for her to come across anyone she knows. There are moments when a familiar face appears in the crowd only to disappear again, leaving her wondering whether her brain is playing some trick. Mostly though, she walks around the city without fear of awkward sightings or uncomfortable reminders, and finds great freedom in the promise of being unknown.

When she taught at school, the river was a physical boundary between her place of work and home. This sense of separation has only intensified over the past three months, so that she now sees the water as a bridgeless expanse, forever separating those two parts of her life. And although Sarah, a colleague who became a friend, is an uncomfortable link back, perhaps it is loneliness that makes her get dressed and go to meet her.

On her way out, she takes the keys from the bowl beside a black and white photograph of her grandparents. She loves this picture of her mother's parents. They are in their twenties, smiling at each other on a sunny beach. Her grandfather is topless in the heat. Her grandmother wears a striped bathing costume, her bobbed hair an impressive deep black. It is a carefree, intimate moment. As she stares at their faces, she tries to reconcile their youthful figures with the older people she knew. Her grandmother, in heavy-rimmed glasses, face flushed, always sitting near the fire, and her grandfather with thinning grey hair, a sadness in his expression, his shoulders hunched.

It is a short walk to Borough Market. She follows the river, turns inland at London Bridge, and crosses onto Borough High Street, entering the market through its green iron gates. People are buying flowers, fresh bread, olives, pastries. For a moment, she thinks of Paris. The flower shops and patisseries, plates piled high with ornate desserts and miniature chocolates.

A taxi from the Gare du Nord. It is a spring day, gusty and bright. The Seine flows silently. Flower boxes filled with trailing plants sit on window ledges. Doors and windows have decorative metal grilles. The vast oval rooms of le Musée de l'Orangerie. Monet's waterlily paintings curved round its walls. Blue and green and gold. Her grandfather, pointing out reflections in the water, the sun flashing through the trees.

By now she is in the open-air market, passing rows of street-food sellers and overflowing bins, then into Southwark Cathedral's courtyard where she finds the little café. She is early and sits at a table near the window. There's a collection of black and white photographs on the walls. Contemporary scenes of bodies lying on pebbles, starkly realistic but with a beauty of their own.

Sarah appears not long afterwards. Her nose and cheeks are flushed from the cold. Heavily clothed, she removes her coat and scarf, revealing a cream jumper tucked into a pair of high-waisted navy trousers. Always dressed in a timeless style, it is her wavy long-bobbed hair, matt red lipstick and heavy textured eyebrows that place her in the present. Stella gazes down at her own dishevelled appearance, the hastily grabbed jumper and faded jeans. Is she even wearing a bra? She cannot remember when she stopped making an effort.

Lovely to see you, Sarah says, looking Stella over kindly. Her concern seems genuine. So how are you?

I'm OK.

You look well, she nods, encouragingly.

Sarah begins to talk about what has happened at school since Stella left, her sadness at no longer seeing her every day. While she speaks, Stella hears the bustle of the market outside, the faint clatter of an overground train in the distance. Sarah falls silent for a moment, then says:

No one feels particularly good about the way you were treated.

And there it is.

The girls still talk about you, you know. They want to know what you're doing.

Stella thinks of how the staff will reframe the reasons for her departure, to minimise the impact of what happened.

Or perhaps they simply won't talk about her. She would prefer that. And as her friend talks as though there is a way back, she nods and smiles, but keeps glancing at the framed photograph on the wall, the girl at work behind the counter. The café is now filling up, brimming with chatter. When she looks back at Sarah, she sees a new expression: pity.

They say goodbye in the cathedral's courtyard.

It's lovely to see you looking so well, Stella. We must do this again. Sarah's words drift off with her into the afternoon.

Stella goes back inside and sits alone in the grand cathedral beneath the Norman arches and the stained-glass windows. There is an installation near the altar: an enormous dark-grey rain cloud hovers mid-air, translucent in sheer fabric. In the silence of this ancient space, she feels consoled, meditative. She realises what her heart has been telling her, that there is a before and an after. A time when words such as struggle and loss seem empty, and a threshold that is crossed after which those words become heavy with meaning. Her heart is beating slowly yet forcefully. Overhead, the cathedral's spires rise high into the winter sky.

*

Early morning. A powerful storm is raging. It has not blown through overnight. It will rain all day. She is reluctant to leave her apartment, but the appointment with her therapist forces her to dress and go outside. In the alleyway leading to his house, she notices that the withered potted plants have gone. In their place, a tall shrub and a young plant, staked with bamboo canes, stand resilient to the heavy downpour and fierce gusts of wind. Their pale green leaves bounce up and down under the weight of the raindrops.

The umbrella has proved useless. It has blown inside out repeatedly on her wind-buffeted walk from the Tube so that her navy mac is sticking to the back of her legs, her long hair blown in the opposite direction to its normal parting. He opens the door and lets her compose herself in his small hallway, her heart still racing despite the calm interior. Then he sits down at the table, tucks his legs under the chair and starts to write, slowly. She admires this simple act.

She finds it hard to settle this morning. She doesn't know if it's the rain-soaked journey, the jostling on the pavements or the busy Underground affecting her ability to be present, or whether there is something different in the room. Whether he is different. She glances around at the artwork, the kitchen, the table. The flowers are shop-bought rather than picked – she has seen a similar bunch in the small supermarket at the end of his road – but everything else seems unchanged.

He asks how she's feeling, what she has thought about since their last session. This is how they always begin, yet today she is unable to concentrate. She tries to focus her attention on his face, his explanations of what they are doing, why they are doing it. She mentions how she felt on the bus, as though her old self has died and that she can no longer trust who she is. He assures her that a wide range of emotions is normal during EMDR, to be expected even, and that she may also experience new sensations in her body.

For me, it was a fierce warmth at the back of my neck.

His uncharacteristic openness takes her by surprise. Until now, he has revealed nothing about himself. For a moment they are no longer patient and therapist. They are simply two people sharing a moment of vulnerability.

He clears his throat and shuffles his papers, aware that the conversation has become personal, intimate even, some professional boundary at risk. When he next speaks, it is with uncharacteristic force.

So, what else has come up for you?

She finds herself talking about her mother, the last few weeks of her life, the physical transformation that was so painful to watch. Stella was at her bedside throughout those weeks, unlike the earlier times which she cannot speak about.

When she gets up to leave, she notices an object in the corner of the room. At first, she thinks it is one of his guitars, until she looks more closely. It is a sitar. Its short bulb-shaped body extending into a long teak neck has been resting against the wall throughout their session.

A bitter wind accompanies her home. It sweeps across the city, ripping through the plane trees, buffeting the leaves. It howls around corners of houses and shops, whips the Thames's surface into black peaks. Alone again, sorrow consumes her. She watches one raindrop after another slide down the bus windows, slipping, pausing, then joining together.

*

Late afternoon. The storm has passed. Brightness gleams weakly on wet surfaces as she makes her way to a yoga class. She loves to feel her body moving and expanding during the flowing practice, the sense of connection with the group. Her therapist is pleased that she likes yoga. It complements the EMDR process, he says, as both therapies relieve imbalances in the nervous system. She sometimes arrives at their sessions with her yoga mat, and purposefully draws attention to it by leaning it against her chair.

The classroom's large windows look out over the square, and her eyes are level with the trees as she practises, their branches black and bare in winter. The teacher wears long filigree earrings that remind her of jewellery in Moroccan street markets. When she places her hand on a student's back, to encourage the softening of a position, her delicate gold bracelets slip down her arm and jangle together with a pleasing sound. She is reminding the class how the moving postures echo the cycles and rhythms of nature. A recurring sequence of beginnings, middles and ends. That we're all in a moment – whether joyous or painful – and that it will change. We can't be attached to it, but we can be gently aligned with it.

As Stella moves through this series of ancient move-ments, their effect begins to deepen and grow within her like a chant. She feels the sensation shifting and changing, as though something is softly releasing, until there is smoothness inside her abdomen, her chest. If she were to describe the feeling to her therapist, she would use an image: a field of fresh snow, or a deep blue sea, vast and still. And at this moment, she hears a gentle voice and what it says is kind, so kind, that it cannot be her own.

I love you.

When the class ends, she rolls up her mat and descends the stairs, passing classrooms filled with literature and art classes. She crosses through the campus onto Tottenham Court Road, tightening the belt of her coat against the cold. Evening has quietened the pavements. People are walking more slowly, pausing at shop windows to look at furniture displays and co-ordinating home décor, organic food and beauty products. Sometimes, she lingers before the windows, feeling an emptiness, a lack, but this evening, she passes by without noticing.

Outside the Underground, workmen are starting to hang lights from the bare trees. Circular ornaments, which will reveal icy patterns and swirls when illuminated. She descends the escalators into the stale air of the Tube, but she is breathing another air. She is thinking of real snow falling on a field, each flake intricately detailed and beautiful. And deep within, her heart softly thuds.

Julia

It is almost dawn. I'm awake early, like you always were, long before your father or sister stirred: their deep slumber had a restorative quality we envied. From where I stand at my open bedroom window, I can see down to the cove and the tumble of black rocks at the base of the cliff. The tide is far out, leaving a brackish, rotting smell of seaweed, but I can still hear the waves. Their distant rhythm soothes me. I imagine you returning from an early morning walk, unfastening the rusty clasp of the gate, and striding across the lawn towards the house. Your long, dark hair is flaring behind you, a strand of it finding its way into your mouth. You tuck it behind your ear but the wind tugs it free almost immediately. I scan your profile, your body, for a sign that the walk has dispersed whatever difficult feeling you awoke with. Sometimes, my maternal intuition allowed me to sense your emotional state even before I saw your crossed arms and heard your fierce, angry steps. But there is no point walking down to you this morning. No point calling out.

I've started embroidering again, during the long
summer evenings, and in the mornings when
I am alone. A repeating pattern of white roses and
wild purple orchids, caterpillars and butterflies,
masses of strawberries. It was inspired by something
I saw at the Kensington Museum when your sister
took me to an exhibition of Tudor and Stuart Fashion.
Among the lace collars and silk costumes, sewn
thickly with jewels, was a small yellow tunic with
puffed sleeves, its tiny proportions adorned with
nature motifs in brightly coloured silks. I told your
sister I would copy the design and embroider
a long roll of fabric for the centre of your bed.
She looked at me hesitantly, then kindly, and said
it was good I was starting something new.

It's not Diana's fault that she is so different from
you, but in that moment, I wished I'd never mentioned the pattern I wanted to sew. She doesn't share
the depth of feeling my work gave you. I could
see the fascination in your face whenever you held
a section of my embroidery, closely examining the
intricate stitches. A moment of peace came over you,
a visible relaxing of your forehead, and whenever
I saw you altered like that, I felt such love for you.

The pattern requires a great deal of concentration. I prefer to work on it alone, especially when I'm at a difficult part of the design or the colours need consideration. Sometimes, I look up to see Louisa watching me closely and wonder whether she resents my project.

The other evening, we were sitting outside on the terrace; it was still warm, still light enough to see the glowing pink cliffs. Louisa was talking about her children. Toby's work for the government and Lily, who is expecting another child. Her grandsons staying at Easter, climbing trees and rock-pooling in the cove. My boy this, my boy that, she kept saying. I nodded and looked up every so often, said a few words, but I was concentrating on my stitches and this brought natural lapses in our conversation. I must have been working on a particularly challenging part, for her chatter suddenly became unbearable. I tried not to show my irritation in the way I snipped at the threads and wound the bundles of silks in my lap before retiring.

I will use a deep crimson for the strawberries and a mixture of different stitches to depict their puckered skins. Do you remember the house we rented near Leith Hill? Perhaps you were too young.

The large garden led directly onto a wooded valley and at the brow of the hill was a fruit farm. We would take long walks over the hill and pass fruit pickers working in the fields. Diana scampered along, not wanting to pause beside the plants bedded on manure, but you dawdled, pulling me back by the hand. You wanted to watch the men picking strawberries and raspberries. One of the workers began to recognise us and smile every time we passed. One day, gently cupping a berry, he snapped its stem and offered it to you. I expected you to hide behind my legs, but you sprang forward and seized it. And that was you, my most sensitive child, yet always able to conceal your anxiety, your timidity from others.

It was soon after we moved to Edwardes Square that you started having nightmares. Something tormented you, some feeling that you couldn't bear. I used to come and wrap my arms tightly around you. I told you there was nothing to worry about, that nobody could harm you, you were safe. I saw, you kept repeating. But what had you seen? I looked all over your room and out of the window and found nothing. Everywhere was silent. In truth, the way you clung to me during those nights consoled me as much as it consoled you. In the early days of my marriage, I had doubts about my new role as wife, but did my best to hide these anxieties from you.

Your father tried to understand your temperament, my darling, but your sensitivity, the sudden flaring of your emotions exasperated him. In later life, he encouraged your artistic ambitions. The painting classes that you took, at the Slade and Royal Academy schools, where you were restless and lacking in inspiration. We bought you all the equipment you needed, but in the end, you preferred photography. I remember your first camera, a large wooden box covered with leather. You captured us in the rooms of our home, outside in the garden. Black-and-white fragments of our lives.

You started posing for your own photographs. A natural model with your long black hair, pale skin, cobalt-green eyes. The camera had a long cable with a rubber bulb at the end to activate the shutter. The early self-portraits are beautiful: images of you with a white parasol, your delicate figure in flowing silk dresses, but the later ones show your face darkened by shadow, or reflected in a mirror with a desolate expression, hair concealing part of your face. I removed those images from your album but couldn't bring myself to throw them away.

Looking back now, I wonder if you had started to hide things from me, even then.

You persevered with painting. In Paris, in Venice. We never discouraged you from travelling. But these European schools too, you found wanting. And each time you came home, I saw a change in you. You became thinner, a sort of emaciation slowly taking you over, as though by losing more and more of yourself, you were edging closer to being the person you wanted to be.

The last time you returned, I looked at you closely for a long time. I hadn't seen you in five months. You were exhausted from travel, and so thin, but there was something else, something in your expression, a kind of weary elation.

The nights are hot here, my love. I sleep with the windows open and sometimes the curtains undrawn. Last night, there was a great yellow moon, glistening on the tops of the pines, the black rippling sea. I drew the curtains, but every time the fabric billowed in the breeze, light came into my room. Eventually, in the early hours, I gave up on sleep. I opened the curtains and sat beside the window, watching the sky become whiter in the east and the sea slowly lighten to blue.

Stella

A cold winter day, the possibility of snow. She sits at the window of her apartment, light spilling from heavy clouds, looking out.

She lives in East London beside a narrow inlet of the Thames. One of the city's lost rivers flowed out here long ago. Now it is a dock, bordered by wharves, filling with water twice a day. Coots paddle about excitedly with twigs in their beaks and swans glide through the waves, untroubled by the swirling plastic bottles and other floating debris. This morning, as she longs for the swans to appear, she's remembering a car journey with her parents. Shifting uncomfortably in the back seat, then suddenly noticing a white expanse through the car window. A mass of curved necks and thick flat bodies reaching into the distance, the ground covered in white feathers. A field of swans. So exquisite, she could almost not bear the sight of it, yet as she remembers her breath catching in her throat, she is unable to separate this memory from that of her mother's fading health, the look in her father's eyes.

He is visiting her on one of his rare trips to London. He will want to walk along the river if the cold allows, to stretch his legs after the journey and perhaps to recapture earlier memories.

A gusty day, her hair blowing in the wind, the water racing past in shades of blue and grey, the gentle ease of her mother by their side.

Her father's journey will have already begun from the old stone rectory where Stella grew up, a house she prefers not to visit. Her mother's hardback books no longer line the study shelves. Unfinished paintings, collages, scraps of fabric and hand-made lace no longer fill the tables in her studio. The cupboards have been emptied of her colourful floral dresses (many with the tags still on), white sandals of different height wedges, wool jumpers smelling faintly of *J'Adore*, the perfume Stella had sprayed all over herself after the funeral. A multitude of moisturisers and pale pink lipsticks, differing ever so slightly in shade or lustre, thrown away. Even the abundance of the garden has been diminished. Old tumbling roses are tightly pruned back, the once carefully tended wisteria stripped from the wall to save the stonework, though in Stella's less forgiving moments, she suspects another person's influence.

He texts when he is downstairs in the lobby. The lift doors open and she takes in his carefully combed grey hair, full for a man of sixty-seven, and the customary V-neck over a navy-and-white checked shirt. He has the face of a man who spends a lot of time in the sun.

Hi, Dad.

They greet each other with a quick hug and her body remembers being carried on his shoulders, feeling his arms prise her from where she'd fallen asleep as a child and gently carry her up to her bedroom. But her mind, her mind won't allow her to forget the later omissions and lapses. The absences.

Pressed together in the confines of the lift, she can smell his breath when he talks and leans away slightly, her head thudding softly against the wall. Since her mother died a year ago, her father seems to be constantly on the move – he has just returned from a week's skiing – and recounting these trips is usually the prelude to any meaningful conversation with her.

Inside her apartment, he settles himself in her chair, crosses one leg over another. He seems slimmer, more groomed perhaps, and now she thinks of it, his clothes smell of a new detergent. She makes him an espresso, places the tiny cup on the table beside him.

Ah, thanks. He lifts it to his mouth, then pauses. So how's it going with, um – ? He takes a sip.

My therapist? she says, and shrugs her shoulders. Useful, I guess. I can talk about things. I can talk about Mum.

She likes to say the word out loud. She remembers Frieda Plath introducing a performance of her mother's poetry at the Southbank many years ago. Sylvia Plath is my mother, not *was,* is. Stella also wants to keep her mother in the present, to affirm her existence. Unlike a possession, her mother can never be purged.

Good, good. He takes another sip of coffee, sets the cup down carefully on the table beside him.

He has offered to pay for her therapy on more than one occasion, preferring to call it 'meetings', but she has absolutely refused. She is determined to pay for it herself. For as long as she can. There are lots of things she doesn't want to tell him. Not just the cost of these 'meetings' and what they discuss, but how she was dismissed from her teaching position, how little she has put by. Once, during an argument, she accused her father of caring only about money, and though this isn't entirely true – Stella knows he recognises the value of pursuing a passion, of finding contentment even – she knows he does care, most of all, about money.

She asks about Anita, a family friend who attended the funeral impeccably turned out (at a time when Stella still slept in her clothes), and then disappeared with her father to Italy shortly afterwards.

She's well, thanks, busy with her social work.

Stella no longer presses him on when their relationship

began, for she assumes they are in a relationship and that it has progressed further than 'companionship'. They are a family where some things are never talked about, and she's beginning to understand the value of this silence.

He rises from his chair, walks over to the window. With a lightly tanned arm, he starts to point out landmarks he knows.

Can you see the bridge from here?

He bends slightly, alters his perspective.

No.

In that moment, it feels like the obscured view is her fault. She idles at the other side of the room, pulling at her sleeve, then reluctantly joins him by the window.

The river flows beneath them as she points out notable features of the area: the different warehouses that used to store wheat, barley, and pungent spices, their brick walls still infused with the fragrance of cinnamon, cardamom, coriander, the cranes that once loaded produce on and off steamboats, now hanging idle on the walls. For though he dislikes talking about the past, *never look back* is his motto, he is interested in local history, especially history he knows. He talks about the City, what it was like when he worked there, where some now-obsolete restaurant or law office used to be. As he speaks, he gesticulates at the silver cityscape on the other side of the river, the vast modern buildings with entire floors that are always lit. She never understood what he did in those buildings, knowing only that he moved from company to company every year or two.

He glances at his watch, then back at his coffee abandoned on the table. She wonders if he is starting to worry about his car parked outside. Or is it being with her that makes him awkward? Stella knows she closely resembles her mother – her aunt always remarks upon it, the same blue eyes with clear black pupils, though hers are a touch greener, the same eager smile, the head tilt when listening – and wonders whether this is why he sometimes avoids looking at her. But when he does allow himself to look, his face is soft, with a tender expression. She doesn't know what he is thinking, only that there is some emotion, of which even he is probably unaware, behind his eyes.

He hesitates then takes a breath.

You know Anita has moved in with me. Well, we're thinking of getting married. It's time, he adds, quickly.

As he explains that he could never have known his life was going to be like this, losing his wife in his sixties, being lucky enough to find love again, all Stella can think is that her father shouldn't be doing this, they shouldn't be having this conversation, none of this should be happening. As she starts to speak, she can almost feel her mother's hand on her arm. It is enough to silence her. When she opens her mouth again, all she can say is:

I'm pleased for you, Dad.

He leans forward and kisses the top of her head.

She wants to say something more, but feels that she might start crying so follows his example in avoiding all that is uncomfortable.

After a moment, she forces a smile and says:

My dad getting married! She playfully hits him on the arm.

Shortly afterwards, they leave her flat and part company on the narrow street where she lives.

Too cold for a walk today, kiddo.

He cannot look her in the eye, and smiles apologetically at the floor. She tightens her mother's oat-coloured scarf, the softest of all the wool she owned, around her neck and nods.

*

She doesn't know how long she stands there before turning and walking down to the river. The wind is cold and she can taste salt, but the water is comforting, the proximity of it, the movement as it races past her. She follows the path which cuts inland between converted warehouses, new-build flats and rows of dockworkers' terraces until the view suddenly opens out to a wide expanse of river. Canary Wharf is to the east and, by some illusion of the river's bend and breadth, the Shard looms tall on the north side, but she is not looking at it. Her attention is drawn to the people walking past, each face striking her so forcefully that it takes her a moment to understand why. It is not that they're threatening. On the contrary, each person looks remarkably familiar or as if, with the slightest shift of their features, they would become someone she knows. The river races with surprising speed, but otherwise nothing else seems strange or out of place. The path, which now runs through narrow cobbled streets, past the old Dickensian pub with its daily changing menu, is just as it should be. As she comes to a small patch of scrubland the path empties. The river flows, but no longer races. She is alone, walking, and that is all that matters.

It is evening when she returns home. Streetlights gleam in the darkness. She crosses the small bridge over the dock and looks up to see one or two lighted windows in her building. Beneath her feet, a swan is resting on the muddy sediment of the riverbed, its long neck and head tucked into its back as it sleeps.

*

The days are getting shorter and shorter as the winter solstice draws near. Daylight is flat, white, short-lived. Next door, the apartment is let. She hears a male voice inside as she waits for the lift. In the evenings, when she approaches her building, she sees the flickering of a television reflected in the window of his apartment.

She lies awake at night, trying to make sense of her life, how it has arrived at this juncture, how she will move it forwards. Nobody is to blame for anything, or perhaps her mother's death is to blame for everything. When sleep comes, it is fitful, her dreams confused. Sometimes she wakes – or dreams she wakes – to hushed voices outside her apartment, the sound of a door closing, her neighbour's nocturnal comings and goings, but she must fall back asleep, for then she is in her childhood bed, whispered voices on the landing, her mother bending down in the darkness and gently pulling the duvet over her.

Memories from long ago are slowly filtering back. Certain images or fragments are as real as the paintings on her therapist's walls, others appear blurry, dark, impossible to decipher. He has asked her to scan back through her life as though watching it in reverse on a big screen. Which images or events leap out? She exhausts her memory until anxiety begins to seep in. She will tell him there is nothing more.

Julia

Diana visited your grave last week. The cemetery was so empty, she said, the deep silence of it stayed with her. There was a small posy of violets on your headstone, each flower carefully arranged. Who has left them? I need to know. I've been looking through your letters from Ceylon searching for a mention of the people you met, anyone with whom you spent the last months of your life. But other than mentioning some friends, Rachel and Christopher in Kandy, you told me only about the island. Of its hills and mountains edged with shadow, the vast dry lagoons, the fierce sun, the ruins at *Thûparâma Dâgba*. How you travelled round the island by bullock cart, passing through walls of trees and into the deep silence of the rainforest. The stillness disturbed only by the rustle of grey monkeys in the treetops or scurrying across the road in front of you.

In your letters, you mention taking many photographs, but I found only one in your trunk: a picture of a young woman with long, uncombed hair, her slender neck turned away from the camera.

You have written *Aletheia* (truth) underneath. It is faded, but I like it that way.

I suppose you were limited in what you could bring back, packing in a hurry before catching the boat from Colombo to Marseilles, the train across France. Gerald has written to tell me that he is coming home at Christmas, taking leave from his diplomatic duties, and will bring your remaining possessions with him. Are there photographs amongst them? It is when I look at your photographs that you feel most alive to me.

At first you didn't know where to place the dark box or how to arrange the sitter, but you persisted, persuading family, friends, or even passers-by whom you spotted from the window to pose before your camera. Your passion, your endless demands made sitting for you an ordeal! Diana remembers having to stay absolutely still, in the exact pose you wanted, for just as long as you required. It took time to achieve the soft, out-of-focus-effect you preferred to the sharp detail other photographers insisted upon.

I remember that time we were discussing your desire to travel, how you sat down among the green velvet cushions in the sitting room, lit another cigarette, and listened to me with a frown on your face. There were fresh flowers on the polished wood table behind you, and light from the window gilded the leaves, the edge of your face. I can see it now, the diffused light, the almost perfectly composed picture.

I understand your concern, Mother, you said, but I don't think there's much to worry about. I know I'll be fine.

It must have been about that time you began coming home late and going straight to your room. You wouldn't tell me where you'd been or simply said, a literature class.

The more I try to find my way back to you, the more distance I feel comes between us. I confess that my mood has dipped lower since coming here, my separation from your grave filling me with a new despair. I went to the village church, hoping to feel your presence, but it was cold, solemn. The light barely shone through the stained-glass windows. It was only when I laid a small wreath of lilies beside a headstone in the graveyard, where large rose hips were casting their shadow onto the stone, and heard the pipping of a bird in the tree, that I felt any connection with you.

It is midsummer with its long days of sunlight.
Louisa and I take late afternoon walks when
the heat has dropped. These last few months have
removed a layer of protective skin, so that the
shriek of gulls overhead startles me and the heat
feels oppressive. Louisa tries to distract me by
talking about the different birds singing in the trees,
describing their habits and peculiarities. She recognises all the coastal flowers and draws my attention
to the gorse and the palm trees now flowering
with a scent of almonds. She loves this country,
has no wish to travel, and yet I yearn to tour now.
To Marseilles or Venice. I have a profound longing
to be alone. You know it has always been my
impulse to seek solitude when things are difficult.

As I look out past the scorched lawn, the yellowing grass, to the treetops and the sea beyond, it is
hard to comprehend how life continues when yours
has ended. What would you have done with it,
my love? What future lay before you?

Earlier today, when I held your silver necklace,
feeling the cold, rigid heart-shaped ornament in
my hand, a keen feeling of you suddenly overcame
me. I felt you in the room, and a sense of lightness,
of profound happiness, settled within me.

And then just as suddenly you left, and grief closed back in. Dark. Impenetrable. I am in the middle of a forest, and must cut my way towards the light.

Stella

There is a lot she does not tell him. The doubt that has shadowed her all her life; the loathing, a secret kind she reserves for herself, and in the grey afternoon light, with his books piled neatly on the shelves behind her, she does not mention the white flower.

From the beginning, he is preoccupied. He puts his coffee on the table more forcefully than usual, runs a hand through his hair several times before sitting down. He looks tired and she wonders what is causing him to sleep badly.

Shall we pick up where we left off?

There is an edge of impatience in his voice.

She places her hands on the table, exhales in readiness, but her bracelet keeps slipping over her wrist, and she glances at him apologetically as she adjusts it. He watches steadily while she pushes the thin gold band along her arm until it tightens against her skin. An uncomfortable moment of silence passes between them.

Ready? he asks, finally.

She nods, closes her eyes, and he begins to tap each hand quickly with a pen. Right and left. Right and left. To stimulate different parts of her brain and move her into a subtly different consciousness. In this new space, the dark blank of her mind begins to open. The first image is faint: a tiny globe of light, like a pearl, that slowly expands into one, two, then three white, softly grooved petals, opening from the centre. A flower, unlike any flower she has seen before, amid glossy-green pointed leaves.

She hears his voice asking what she sees, and the flower distorts and changes, becomes a white dress her mother is wearing. It must be spring or early summer for she has no coat. Her mother is laughing, then walking away, and it doesn't occur to Stella that she might follow her. A warm sensation in her sternum. She feels out of breath. Is it possible to experience heartache as a physical pain? He allows her to stay with this sensation for a moment before guiding her back to her calm place. Once she is breathing more slowly, he explains the process again.

EMDR seeks to shift how memories sit inside us, he says. An experience can get stuck and dominate our psyche in a way it shouldn't.

She forces a smile. You mean I'm doing this to myself.

No, he says, leaning back in his chair. It's quite unconscious. It matters less what you see, more the thoughts and emotions you have when seeing it.

He places his hands on the edge of the table, appears to be thinking for a moment.

I find it interesting you chose to study drama.

The change of subject takes her by surprise. She thinks of the drama studio at school. Full of textures and diffused light, with dusty props on shelves, assorted costumes, velvet curtains falling onto the floor in heavy purple folds. On stage, she could assume a character that wasn't her own. Acting often felt more real than the world to which she had to return.

I enjoyed it at school, she says.

At the end of their session, he disappears for a moment, then comes back wearing his coat.

I'll walk out with you.

He has a hair appointment immediately after their session. It is the only time the salon has available, he explains, a touch apologetically. As they walk through the narrow alleyway and onto the main road, he is mostly silent, looking into shop windows or at the pavement. Sometimes he is a step or two ahead and she has to quicken her pace to catch up. The longer they walk, the more she is unnerved by his presence and how his body feels oddly cold beside her. She is relieved when he says goodbye in front of the salon and goes inside.

In the weeks that follow, she cannot shake the image of the white flower from her mind. Like the rise and fall of waves in front of her eyes long after looking at the sea. The flower surfaces in her dreams, sometimes blossoming, its delicate petals unfurling from curved buds, or drifting and scattering like snow. She searches the internet when she should be looking for jobs and becomes obsessed with finding its likeness, if only in a photograph or drawing, intent on discovering a name, a genus, a habitat, anything to help her identify it. No flower resembles it, and she is too embarrassed to ask a florist for she can hardly explain how she saw the image, let alone find the words to describe it. She visits the British Library and spends days with piles of botanical manuals, floral encyclopaedias, travelogues by famous plant-collectors with tales of risky expeditions to Burma, China, Sri Lanka, Himalaya. Opening one book after another, she reads only a few paragraphs before turning to the colour plates at the centre. She is transfixed by the images rendered in delicate watercolour. In the evenings, she emerges, briefly disorientated, from the glaring brightness of the library straight onto a dark Euston Road.

One evening, on her bus journey home, she sits behind a mother and daughter. The daughter is a similar age to herself, the mother in her late sixties or early seventies. They are planning the next few days: Christmas shopping on

Oxford Street, the pre-Raphaelite exhibition at the Portrait Gallery. The mother gently tucks a loose strand of her daughter's hair behind her ear and Stella has to look away.

Outside the sky is dark, starless. There are reminders of the season: glittering trees in shop windows, strings of lights looped along balconies, and beyond the lights, Stella sees her own mother's hand, resting gently on flowers and shrubs in a garden, the leaves springing back after her touch. That hopeless desire is always present, to feel her mother's touch once more, the tightness of her embrace, heart resting against heart. When she wakes the following morning, it is with a physical longing, not just for her mother, but for something she cannot identify. She drinks an espresso in her empty kitchen and heads out to the library.

Not long after that evening, she comes across an old postcard in a reclamation shop off Maltby Street. It is a black and white photograph of St Paul's Cathedral, post-marked December 1911. There are waggons with shaggy ponies in the foreground, groups of men in caps standing beside the steep white steps. On the other side, a brief note to an addressee in Devon:

I hope you have a good Christmas and I trust you will feel all right when it is over!

She fixes it to the front of her fridge with a magnet she bought from the Tate. An image of Georgia O'Keefe's Jimson Weed/White Flower No.1. It is not Stella's white flower, but that does not matter.

*

During one of her walks, Stella discovers a patch of scrubland out east. She takes to following the track, which always leads her to a bench, overgrown by weeds and wildflowers, facing the river. The water birds are silent here. Inland gulls settle on the water in small groups. Three weeks have passed since she first saw the white flower, four weeks since her father's visit, when she walked along this path and her sorrow made her shiver. She finds herself thinking of her mother, standing at a window in a room full of light. It is the kitchen of their family home; the light in it, her mother's presence.

Recently the dreams have changed, no longer filled with the white flower. She is walking in deep green, broken here and there by sunlight. Moss covers the ground, dotted with little yellow flowers. Sword-like leaves press in on her, and the light dims as she advances. She hears creaking, sighing sounds, and the occasional cry of an animal. Her dress appears startlingly white in the darkness. She has the sense that she must keep walking, deeper into the rainforest – to a destination that is always just out of reach – and each morning she wakes with the hazy memory of a path, crossed with fallen branches covered in thick creepers, and the feeling of something unfinished and incomplete.

Her therapist suggests support meetings for grief, so she pretends she is feeling much better until one afternoon, driven by annoyance with herself, she leaves the apartment and walks to an address in Spitalfields. In the last light of the day, she crosses Tower Bridge. The dark river flows endlessly beneath her, and up ahead, she sees the City's buildings, silhouetted against the fading sky. She walks on past redbrick-fronted offices on Commercial Street, hotels on the edge of the financial district, independent coffee shops, until the lights of Spitalfields market indicate her turning on the right. For a moment, she is tempted to enter one of the shops glittering in the dusk, but something compels her to keep walking.

The meeting is held in a community room on the corner of Hanbury Street next to a Vapes & E-cigs newsagent with its name illuminated in red letters down the side of the building. She waits until the previous occupants, teenage girls from an Islamic studies group, stream out of the front door, accompanied by two teachers. One or two girls giggle as they pass her by.

Stella follows a young woman inside. She has long, dark hair of a single length, full lips, bright oval eyes. An open and expressive face, reminiscent of an actress Stella once saw on stage. The woman rests her violin case against a chair in the middle of the room, nods at one or two people. Stella sits down in the nearest seat, and decides against removing her coat. Soon, the room is filled with people of all different ages. After a few minutes, a woman with short grey hair, wearing a purple velvet skirt, clears her throat and stares expectantly at the group. Her cheeks are flushed and she fiddles with a tangle of gold chains at her neck.

Welcome everyone. My name is Helen. Is there anyone new tonight? Stella opens her mouth to speak as the man sitting to her left raises his hand.

Hi there, my name is David. I've recently lost my partner.

The group says welcome in unison.

Stella's heart is throbbing in her chest. She speaks quickly next:

Hi, I'm Stella, I was recommended to come here.

Her welcome seems less enthusiastic, but the young woman meets her eyes with a smile that seems genuinely warm. There is an open notebook on her lap and she is holding a pen in her hand.

The meeting begins with everyone discussing how they feel this evening, or 'getting current', as Helen describes it.

While each person speaks in turn, the young woman, who had introduced herself as Anne, writes vigorously in her book. By the time the man with sad eyes next to Stella begins to share, her heart is pounding. When her turn comes, she talks fast, summarising her mother's death and what has happened since as dispassionately as she can. Afterwards, the room feels unnaturally quiet and her cheeks are scalding. Anne has stopped writing and is staring at Stella with her hand resting at the side of her face. The sleeve of her thick navy jumper is pushed back to the elbow, revealing a scalloped, wave-like tattoo on her wrist.

After the meeting, Stella heads back towards Spitalfields market and glimpses Anne up ahead. In a dark shapeless coat, long hair tucked into the collar, violin case by her side. Stella deliberately slows her pace, but cannot avoid catching up with her at the pedestrian crossing. Standing beside her for a moment, she pauses, then says, Hi.

Anne turns, smiles. Oh, hi there, she replies, then faces the road, with no apparent desire to initiate conversation. Instead, she gazes up at the moon, full and clear in the sky, perfectly at ease.

I'm sorry about your sister, Stella says, breaking the silence.

The young woman had talked about her sister in the meeting. The ovarian tumour following repeated IVF cycles.

Driving late at night to satisfy her sister's chemotherapy food cravings. Frantically returning with biscuits or a take-away burger only to find her sister vomiting, no longer able to stomach food. The long battle that her sister had fought bravely until, eventually, she was defeated.

Thanks, she says quietly, still gazing at the moon. I'm sorry to hear about your mother. She turns towards Stella. Was it your first meeting?

Stella nods.

They help, Anne says, beginning to cross the road as the pedestrian lights turn green. Talking about it has a particular power – she pauses, as if trying to define the power. It doesn't stop hurting, but you learn to contain it. To get on with living.

A gust of wind blows the scarf from around her neck and she takes a long time rearranging it to her satisfaction as they walk along Bishopsgate. Raising her eyes to the sky once more, she is silent for several moments, then says:

People think the sky is the same everywhere, but my sister always said the stars were brighter in the North. I miss seeing the stars here.

Outside Liverpool Street station, the young woman stops, seems to hesitate, prompting Stella to ask if she is going inside. She nods, then says:

Can I give you my number? I'd feel happier if you had it. Call me if you ever need to talk. I'm Anne, by the way, she adds, reminding Stella of her name in case she'd missed it in the meeting.

It feels overly intimate but Stella saves her number in her phone, touched by this gesture of kindness.

Maybe see you next week, Anne says, then descends the escalators amidst crowds of office workers, the flash of her red scarf disappearing last.

Stella reflects on the evening as she walks home. The meeting was comforting, bonding. The people had seemed to know what she was feeling, if only some of it, and she'd felt calmer towards the end. Exhaling deeply, she looks up at the sky and allows herself to imagine stars gleaming in the darkness above.

Later, when she reaches for her phone – kept in readiness by the bed, a habit from when her mother was alive – she scrolls through her contacts. Anne's name comes up first. She falls asleep as the last commuter train clatters distantly past.

Julia

This morning, I was convinced someone was
standing at the end of my bed, watching me sleep.
I sat up against the pillows, half-awake, and reached
for my spectacles, but there was no one there.
As I lay back down, all I could hear was the sound
of birds in the garden, the distant waves breaking
on the shore. Perhaps I'd imagined it, my imagination
running away with me again. After a few moments,
I rose from my bed, took my silks, scissors, and
thimble downstairs and started work in the first light.
I'm sewing the monogram of your initial in a soft
coral thread, interwoven with green leaves. H for
Helena. The name I chose for you. Your father wanted
Clarissa after his mother, but I liked Helena, a name
uniquely yours.

My firstborn child. Your father and I married in
spring and after an appropriate pause, everyone
began looking at me expectantly. Yet each month,
the familiar dragging sensation in my stomach.
Walking along the Strand one day, I saw a crumpled newspaper in the gutter. It curled and flapped

in the passing traffic, and just for a moment, when the road was quiet, I glimpsed the image of a baby on one of its pages. The doctor confirmed I was pregnant the following month, but I already knew. You, my darling, were inside me. I finally understood what people meant when they said there is nothing like carrying your first child. Yet from birth, you were different from how I'd imagined, with your long limbs and fair hair that quickly turned dark. It seemed impossible that a child like you had come from me. Only later did I feel that when looking at you, I was really looking at myself, that the dissatisfaction I felt was not with you but with some aspect of my own character that I saw in yours. Perhaps that's why writing to you was difficult. I found it hard to lie. My last letter to you in Ceylon never arrived, I don't know why, and was sent back to me. I keep it here in my sewing basket:

My darling, you must forgive this short letter. You know I'm not much of a hand at letter writing. Everything is quiet in London. We are in that bleak part of the year, the final plunge into darkness, though I think it is the darkness of early spring as we transition from winter. Your father and I met your cousin Lina for lunch last week and we walked back through

the park. I felt the earth teeming with buds and bulbs,
though not a green leaf showed. Your Aunt Cassandra
is now out of hospital and recovering from flu at home.
I shall perhaps do what I can to visit and make her more
comfortable. I think that's all the news. Please write to
Diana. I know I keep saying this, but she would like to
hear from you.

Your loving mother

Sometimes, I fear you are becoming something you were not, that my memories will fade, and I'll be left with a daughter I can no longer recognise. In truth, I find it hard to remember who I was, before I became a mother, before I was married. I haven't mentioned this to your father. There is so much I cannot tell him.

I have asked Diana to buy a book from Hatchards and post it to me. A new edition of a travel narrative set in Asia, featuring Ceylon, reviewed in *The Times*. It has been republished with additional photographs made possible by advances in printing. How ingenious these people are! When I showed Louisa the review, she gazed at me for a few moments with a slightly puzzled look on her face, then smiled and peered over my shoulder at the article.

I must press on now with the bedspread, for she'll
be down soon. It's not progressing as fast as I'd
hoped. My hands are starting to ache, especially
when I am sewing. It must be my arthritis. I have
to stay the needle in the linen for a moment, take
short breaks, stretch my fingers apart and wait for
the pain to subside, but I will finish this section.
I will complete the H in long and short stitch,
the green leaves that tightly bind it, before Louisa
comes in and makes demands on my day.

Stella

The flower. It comes to her with a clarity she finds astonishing. The whiteness, the tilt of its petals, the purity. She sees it on her mat during yoga, in the gold halo of the teacher's candles, each night when she closes her eyes before sleep. Walking through the city, her eyes find floral images on advertising boards, the spines of books in shops. She notices a single rose blooming out of season in the park.

Flowers filter into her dreams at night, blossoming mysteriously around her. In the morning, as the layers of sleep fall away, she is always walking through rainforest. Endless trees, spiralling leaves, vast bamboo shoots. The heat is tearing, fierce. This lush, green world to which she returns, night after night, is beginning to feel more real than the life she wakes to. During the day, her body remembers sweating in the heat, despite the cold London air around her. She hears creaking and sighing among the city's streets, the rustling of leaves. The forest – or perhaps it is winter – is leaving its physical mark on her. She looks down to see her hands are wrinkled, the skin flaking and peeling like the bark of a tree, then beyond her own flesh, she sees the skin on her mother's face, thin and shrunken, and those pale blue eyes, with the inner luminosity of her final days.

Late December. A light powdering of snow settles across the capital, while in the countryside, heavy flakes fall on fields and lanes. People stagger from buses carrying Christmas gifts. The last office workers amble across a deserted London Bridge.

Two days before Christmas Eve, she finds a card in her letterbox. Her new neighbour is having a party. He apologises in advance for any noise and invites her to drop round. His name, James Manning, is embossed at the top of the card in black italic letters. It is the customary polite gesture and of course she will not go, but she is curious about this James, known only to her by the slamming of his door late at night, the rumble of voices, sometimes more distinctly that of a woman, outside his door.

She attends another support meeting and finds she listens more intently. Everyone has their own experience, yet there are also shared moments: watching a body journey towards its end, believing that a loved one will be granted a pain-free death, the intense longing that Stella can feel palpably in the room. She is disappointed that Anne doesn't attend but feels comfortable in the group and speaks more confidently, with only a gentle nudge at her heart when she does.

On returning home, she ascends slowly in the lift, hearing the sound of people talking loudly as she approaches her floor. The doors open just as her neighbour emerges from his apartment to welcome guests inside. She has forgotten about the party, hopes to walk past unnoticed.

Hey, he calls out, I'm James – can I tempt you in for a drink?

He is smiling at her, clapping the back of a male friend passing through his doorway. She has a moment to consider while cries of greeting erupt from inside. Obeying some impulse she will question later, she finds herself nodding.

His apartment is filled with people laughing and talking. The heat is tremendous and the windows on the other side of the room are covered in condensation. A couple are sitting on the ledge, leaning out, smoking. There are men in suits and ties, women in scant colourful tops. She is conscious of her shapeless cream sweater, her faded old jeans and stands awkwardly, taking a sip of the wine he gives her. Alcohol warms her throat, then moments later her stomach. James starts to say something, but other guests arrive and he goes to greet them. She takes another sip of wine and feels her body relax. At that moment, laughter ripples through the room and she looks around, tries to introduce herself to some people nearby, but the room is too noisy and after a moment, she sits on the edge of a sofa and sips her wine alone.

Her neighbour is busy circulating. She watches how each group break off what they are saying when he approaches, eager to talk to him. One woman hits him affectionately on the arm. He is well-groomed, with a face that is lively, playful, almost too young for the neat haircut, the city shirt, the commanding role of host.

Shortly afterwards, a man with curly blonde hair introduces himself to her. She can't really hear what he is saying and pretends to listen with a strained smile on her face. From what she can make out, he is mocking James and their other work colleagues, who are just out of earshot. She does not find him funny. In fact, he appalls her. He catches the eye of someone behind her, grins, and is still grinning, almost leering, when he looks back at her. James walks past with a bottle, offers it to her. She glances at her watch, then holds out her glass.

Her perception of time has ruptured. She is aware only of things having happened. She no longer has her coat, her bag. Faces are damp and pink, pinker than when she arrived. Her sweater seems to have fallen off one shoulder. When did that happen? At some point she is being grabbed and kissed on the mouth. She likes the taste of him, or is it perhaps the taste of whisky, and leans into the warmth of this other body.

Sensations and darkness converge. The nearness of another awakens her from blackout, the feel of his hand sliding onto her hip, slipping further. Instinctively, she reaches back.

*

The next morning, she is on the far side of a bed, can hear the slow, steady breathing of another person. Slipping from under the sheets – crisp, luxurious– she reaches for her underwear and clothes and finds her bag in the lounge which smells of smoke, of people. While she is dressing at the front door, a car alarm sounds in the street outside. It is only after she has shut the door and crossed the small communal area to her apartment that he stirs.

*

Christmas arrives. She stares out at scant patches of illumination among the dark apartment windows opposite. People have left for the holidays. Turning around, she looks at her small flat. It is empty, undemanding, yet strangely comforting. She arranges a bunch of pink hellebores and ivy with dark berries on the table, lays out a meal of smoked salmon, chopped dill, sourdough bread, a sticky toffee pudding for one. She feels as if she is presiding over a still life arrangement, but the minimal mess of this Christmas suits her.

In the late afternoon, she has a phone call with her father. He sounds tired. Anita's family are due to arrive shortly. Stella can hear a food processor grinding in the background, water running in the sink, the sound of an oven door opening and closing with force.

You must come home next Christmas.

Maybe, Dad.

We want you here, Stella, with us.

She hears Anita's voice from the kitchen, her father mouthing something in reply.

Dad, I'll let you go.

No, it's OK. I've got time. Look, I – oh, there's the doorbell –

I'll let you go.

Miss you, darling.

Miss you, too.

Outside the window, sleet begins to fall, reminding her of snowstorms long ago, the joy of Christmas and school holidays. She sees her mother moving around the kitchen in a burgundy jumper under her apron, black trousers. Every so often, her mother pauses to read a recipe and take out more ingredients from the overcrowded fridge.

And now she is being lifted onto a chair. Her mother stands behind it, resting her chin on Stella's shoulder, reading the recipe out loud and following the instructions with her finger. There is pearly pink polish on her nail, a faint smell of perfume – sweet, floral. Her voice is gentle in Stella's ear.

Sometime in the early hours, the sleet stops and a few stars appear in the dark sky. It becomes colder still. Over the next few days, the air temperature drops below zero. There are warnings of heavy snow in the countryside. The cold air makes her head ache when she goes outside. Her therapist is working the week between Christmas and New Year, says he's available if she would like to meet.

When she walks in, he looks at her with concern and asks if she is all right. There is a tone of sensitivity in his voice she hasn't heard before. Glancing down at her appearance, she wonders what has alarmed him. She is perhaps thinner: her jeans are looser at her waist; tops that gently hugged her curves a few months ago now hang empty around her chest and arms. It is not intentional, this weight loss, at least she is not aware of having willed it, though she never is.

Another winter, the fields behind her family home frozen with snow. Every time her mother placed her arms around Stella, she found her smaller. In the following months, Stella had gradually allowed herself nourishment and begun to fill out. And many years later, it would be Stella's turn to be shocked by her mother's shrinking body, her emaciation, her frailty. She had held her mother, desperate to give back to her whatever had enabled her own body to heal itself, yet as hard as she had willed it, it was impossible.

He asks about her Christmas, leaves her to bring up the obvious void. She confides that she has felt her mother's presence. In her apartment. A sudden, though not startling awareness of her mother being close, inside and outside herself, everywhere and nowhere. What she doesn't say is that she is finding it harder to remember her mother's voice, the rising and dropping intonation of her speech. The expiration of time had deleted her mother's voicemails and though Stella was happy to lose some of them (I'm fine darling, the doctor just thinks – or, the results look good, I'm going to fight this!), she regrets not thinking to record her mother's voice, though she wonders whether to listen to it now would be ill-advised, macabre even.

Has anything else come up for you?

Oh, no, not really – I mean – no more than I've already told you.

She picks up a hardback book from his table, flips absentmindedly through the pages. It feels like a prop, as though she's acting a part. She won't mention the party, or what happened afterwards. The sex feels oddly disloyal to him, and while she has started to tell him more intimate things, she has never mentioned a partner, a boyfriend, her sexual relationships. She has stopped – for the most part – anaesthetising herself with unhelpful things. Exhaling, she places the hardback on the table, beside the flowers, the candle and its halo of light.

An icy wind cuts through her on the walk back to the Tube. She thinks of her parents, of how they had cared for each other throughout their lives. Her father driving her mother to every hospital appointment, staying determinedly by her side, supporting her, if only by his physical presence. And how, after her mother, Stella has never allowed anyone to take care of her. She has never felt able to entrust that role to anyone else.

*

They have agreed to meet on the steps outside St-Martin-in-the-Fields. Stella is already late by the time she finally exits the Underground at Charing Cross and hurries along the Strand towards Trafalgar Square. But maybe her haste is unnecessary. She has a feeling that Anne will appear in her own time, regardless of when the concert starts and of the arrangements they have made.

As it turns out, Anne is already outside the church, talking to a male friend. She smiles, her eyes widening with pleasure, when she catches sight of Stella walking towards them. The friend leaves just before Stella arrives.

Hi, Anne says.

Hi. Stella touches Anne's arm lightly, affectionately. Thanks for suggesting this.

No problem. Here's your ticket.

Stella takes it from her and notices the violin case in her other hand. Anne appears to clasp the handle tighter and says:

Ready to go in?

Stella nods, and follows Anne through the double glass doors into the church's vast interior. All along one side are great arched windows, and, overhead, immense chandeliers are suspended from the vaulted ceiling. It is a grand setting for a concert, yet also intimate, softly lit by hundreds of candles. They find their seats among the wooden pews, a few rows from the front. The programme marking her place has an image of a night sky on the cover and the words, *City Lights: A performance by St Martin's Strings.*

Anne is content to sit in silence, her long black coat falling over the pew in deep folds. She is studying the pulpit on her left, an ornate structure in dark, lustrous oak, elaborately carved with shells, wooden leaves and vines that trail around the balustrade and down to the floor. Stella is about to initiate conversation when a quartet of men and women appear at the front of the church, dressed in black. They bow and take their seats behind music stands. There is a pause as they settle, lift their instruments, then begin.

Stella has heard the concerto many times before, yet it is different this evening, exhilarating, somehow rejuvenated by the church's acoustics. The next piece opens with a solo violin. Stella glances at Anne who sits perfectly still throughout, her full lips pressed together, her eyes watching every sweep of the bow. At the end, the musicians put down their instruments and a man takes his seat at the piano. He has changed into a black suit, but Stella immediately recognises him as the person talking with Anne earlier. She looks down at the programme. Quiet Streets – composed and performed by Gabriel Szabó.

He begins to play and, at first, she watches the way his body moves – his head, his back, his feet – and how his fingers pause on certain chords, drawing out the reverberations. She finds herself exhaling deeply and closing her eyes to better follow the gentle ascents and falls of the notes, the sound passionate yet controlled. She begins to anticipate the allegros, the rhythm of the music, as if it is an echo of something she has heard before. Yet as the notes simultaneously waver and climb, she hears something else, something inside the music itself: a deep silence. She feels a gentle warmth in her sternum, then in the stillness, she senses the soft, peaceable sound of another's presence. It is quiet, gentle and so close, it could be within her. She doesn't want the pianist to stop, but as the final note lingers and he turns towards the audience, the sensation recedes so lightly that she's unaware it has left until Anne touches her shoulder and smiles.

By the end of January, a gold light has broken through the misty white sky. London is crowded again after the holidays. On milder mornings, there is a faint smell of new growth in the air. Ducks and coots swim in pairs along the river. She senses the city's revival, wants to share in it.

A book she has ordered from the British Library finally arrives from long-term storage. She imagines it being summoned from a vast isolated building with shelf upon shelf of books, boxes bulging with biographies and yellowing manuscripts. From the desk in the Rare Books & Music room, she collects the hardback book, covered in fern-green material with the image of a gold temple inlaid on its cover. She takes the book carefully and carries it to her desk, feeling the weight and age of it in her hands.

Julia

Rising early again this morning, just before six,
I made some strong coffee and ate a little sponge
cake left over from yesterday. The backdoor key was
easy to find, in a pewter tankard above the range,
and I let myself out before anyone else was awake.
The air was fresh and damp. Early daylight cast
shadows across the lawn, the coastal path, and
beyond, the sea was silver with a line of white mist
at the horizon. The world had a strange, dream-like
quality. Climbing down the wide steps, I found the
beach beautifully desolate. Purple-pink pebbles
stretched away on all sides and the vast emptiness
made me feel dizzy. I had not been back here since
that first time with Louisa.

As the light grew and the mist began to clear,
I saw a tiny boat far out at sea. In the stillness,
I could just hear the chug-chug of its engine and
the shrieks of gulls circling overhead. It made me
imagine you, my love, lying in that boat on the
Indian Ocean. You wrote to me about it. A voyage
to the northern part of the island. For two days,
you lay on a mattress with the sun beating down on

your face. The coast was obscured by a layer of mist for most of the way, but when it lifted, you saw hordes of white water lilies near the shore. You described the need to get away, to feel cleansed after months at the cottage. It was a curious thing to say. Your letters were becoming increasingly disturbed by then and I didn't know what to make of them.

As I stood on the beach, a gentle breeze picked up and I thought you were whispering in my ear, your lips so close that I could have touched you. I felt a peace I had been craving all week, but as the wind strengthened and began to whip stray hairs around my face, the moment was gone and suddenly I had to leave. I turned from the sea and hastened up the beach, pebbles crunching and sliding under my feet. Every so often I stumbled, slipping on the damp stones beneath me.

*

The flies are becoming a problem. They come inside and die on the windowsill, or lumber slowly along the ledge and fall onto the carpet. We keep the windows closed, yet somehow, they still get in. I hear their constant humming from the alcove where I sit, embroidery on my knee, hidden from sight. I have felt angry this week, and have struggled to contain it. Perhaps it is the constant hum of flies and the close summer air or perhaps it's because I find myself returning to the past and remembering things against my will.

Louisa is in Honiton this morning so I can sew here alone, in the clear summer light, but as steadily as I try to pass the needle in and out, in and out of the white silk fabric, my mind is racing. I cannot get a grip on my thoughts. I cannot force them away. Earlier, when Rose, the housemaid, found me in the alcove, she looked at me suspiciously. It's an expression I've grown accustomed to seeing, though my cheeks still redden. For a moment she stared at my embroidery with a distracted smile on her face, then remembering the letter she had for me, placed it on the table beside the newspaper and left.

There's not much in the news. Louisa insists on buying *The Times*, a paper I know you disliked, with its relentless promotion of British interests abroad. There's a story about an English police official in Ceylon, tried for corruption and obtaining money under false pretences. I moved the vase of lilies and flattened the paper on the table to better see his face, the small eyes, the rather chilling smile. I sense an arrogance in his expression which would have repelled you. I'm reading all this into a photograph, of course, which is quite wrong of me, but then you could also be judgmental. Once you saw a politician you disliked on the front of the newspaper and ripped the page in half. You were making a point, I now see, of asserting yourself in opposition to something, that need in each of us to pit ourselves against an adversary, but at the time I struggled to reconcile your behaviour with the little girl I knew. I remember, too, that your hands were stained greyish-blue from the photographic chemicals and the different processes you were experimenting with. It must have been around that time that you had work accepted to the Photographic Society's annual exhibition. I've kept the pamphlet all these years, stowed it safely somewhere. I must find it when I go home.

You wanted to travel to the exhibition by omnibus even though I would gladly have paid for a cab. You'll enjoy it, you said. The bus was crowded and I wasn't used to the juddering engine, the lurching and stopping, but then the elevated view began to distract me. For the first time, my eyes were level with the upper windows of buildings and in the afternoon light, the glass shone with gold and pink reflections. I remember being struck by how beautiful it was.

Near Westminster Bridge, I turned to look at you. You were staring at the river towards St Thomas' Hospital, deep in thought. I wanted to say something. We were so close, I needed only to incline my head to speak in your ear, but the bus lurched forward and I had to put out a hand on the rail to steady myself. As we crossed the bridge and headed south, more and more passengers alighted so that at the final stop, we were the only ones left. On the pavement, you paused for a moment and looked up and down the empty street. I couldn't tell whether you were concerned about something, or whether you were simply trying to find the way.

The photographs you exhibited were peculiar, bluish in tone. A sequence of five images displayed in a straight line across a white wall. You had depicted yourself taking a self-portrait, that much I could understand, but your face was obscured. You had turned away from the camera so that it captured only the back of your head. You were choosing yourself as the subject, though a subject who refused to be portrayed. I glanced at you, hoping you would explain, but you seemed disappointed by my reaction, or perhaps had already dismissed what I was about to say. You were staring straight ahead, biting your lip, your face a little pale. Perhaps you found it hard to confront your own work.

There were other photographs, more unusual, more macabre. In one, a young girl was stretched out on a bed against a black backdrop. Her face was fragile and deeply shadowed. She was a model, though the realism of it was still shocking, and I told you so. You reminded me that artists have depicted dying images for centuries. You were right, of course, but I cannot remember my reply. What I do remember is the argument when we came to leave. Some of the exhibitors were grouped together outside and you went up to speak with them. As I watched you, the only female in the group, deep in conversation, the wind was moving the top of a nearby tree. A single leaf detached itself and fell ever so slowly onto the ground behind you and in that pause, that almost suspended moment, I was struck by how mature and confident you'd become, as if it were only then being revealed to me. But then your voice rose as you began talking angrily. Whatever one of the men said in response caused an uneasy ripple of laughter in the group and silenced you. When you strode back to me, face flushed with annoyance, you shook your head and led me away.

As we sat together on the bus journey home, I remember thinking how little I knew of your male friends. There was someone in Salisbury to whom you wanted to stay close, and you seemed more interested in him than in anyone else. He went away to serve in the army but you found ways of staying in touch. Diana told me you planned to follow him abroad, though nothing came of it. I didn't have the right to ask. In fact, I would have found that conversation uncomfortable, but like so many things, we will never have the chance to speak of it. Was there someone else, my love? Someone in Ceylon? Is that why you left the cottage so suddenly?

I've been reading the travelogue Diana sent me. I open it at random, let my finger glide down the page, then stop:

In and out amid the multitudes go the flower sellers. The air is heavy with the sharp fragrance of temple-flower. It haunts all the shrines of Lanka with its pungent, uplifting scent. Every vihara or dagaba has its gnarled and ancient tree crowned by clusters of these holy flowers.

I keep the book in my embroidery bag. Last night I left it in the sitting room and when I came down this morning, it had been moved, or at least opened, as some of the pages were creased. And just as I was gazing at them, a distressing memory came back. A few days after you returned home to us. Your fever already advanced. You were lying in your childhood bed, struggling to speak. You put your hand out and touched the other pillow, wanting me to lie down beside you, like when you were young. I would read you a story until you fell asleep, then gently untangle my arm from under you. But I had no book and you were no longer a girl and I couldn't bear to feel again the intense pleasure it would give me.

I wished to be alone today. I yearned for the peace and quiet of solitude, but I was wrong. Solitude is not quiet nor is it peaceful.

Stella

Early morning, before daylight. The river flows smoothly, not yet disturbed by the commuter boats. Lying in bed, on the edge of sleep, her mind casts back and forth between forest paths and starry blossoms, to pages of neatly written manuscript in the British Library. Gradually, she becomes aware of a voice singing. Restrained, exquisite. It is so beautiful her body feels held within its notes, as though floating in warm water. She hears a pigeon cooing from a tree, the post van pulling up outside with the radio blaring. As sounds converge with memories, she sees the drawn curtains of her childhood bedroom, a shadow of the window frame on the linen weave. A white painted cupboard stands dimly in the corner. The singing is indistinguishable from these images, yet the more intently she listens, the more distant it becomes.

Rising from her bed, she takes a few steps, pauses, listens. The sound seems to be coming from her kitchen. As she approaches, the floor becomes warmer, smoother under her bare feet, her body strangely light, the fabric of her nightdress moving softly against her skin. The tune quivers, hesitates, and she pauses again, stays perfectly still but then, after a moment, it continues, more expressive, confident, and louder than before. As she turns the corner and enters the kitchen, the singing stops abruptly. Tears come to her eyes.

Always the same. The first time she woke with it, she thought she'd fallen asleep with her earpods in: the sound seemed to be coming from inside her. Never obtrusive, it materialises softly, unexpectedly. And when it stops, the air surrounding her seems to loosen, disperse, and noises from the outside world begin to filter in. An ambulance siren, a taxi arriving outside, the city waking around her.

*

The days are becoming longer. Daffodils flower in the parks and encircle the base of trees, yet winter clings on. It is un-usually cold. Arctic air blasts the east side of the country. She returns to the steps of St Martin's a few times, but does not go inside. One evening she hears choral music, a beau-tiful medley of tones and voices, through the glass windows. She listens and remembers, smiles.

Sometimes, after waking early, she sits in her lounge with an espresso, searching for jobs online. Her savings are almost gone and this blank on her C.V. will need explain-ing. Too lengthy for compassionate leave or a respectable break between careers. She doesn't want to go back to teaching. She wants to forget, to move on. Tapping a pen against her teeth, she finds herself gazing at Georgia O'Keefe's flower on the fridge while she waits for the sound of her neighbour's door opening and closing, the lift being summoned, then descending, before leaving her apartment for the library.

She has hardly seen her neighbour since Christmas. They have deftly negotiated their shared hallway. Only once have they run into each other. He was coming back up in the lift and they came face to face as the doors opened. Can you wait a moment? He'd asked, rushing past her into his apartment, leaving her pressing the hold button, wishing she'd taken the stairs. He must have been late, she reasoned, unable to wait for the lift to return empty. A moment later, he reappeared, and they descended together. She kept her eyes down, counting off the floors. Occasionally, she felt him looking at her. When he spoke, he was overly polite. How've you been? This lift is so slow! At the ground floor, he made an extravagant gesture of holding the doors open for her, and then she was outside, relieved to be alone. She feels slightly shameful when she remembers sleeping with him, then angry at herself for rising to the old patriarchal narrative. It was an act of pure lust, that's all. The need to not feel or think for an evening. To have a break from herself. It was an aberration. That's all. No longer a pattern.

*

Day after day, she sits at a desk in the British Library with a pile of gold-wreathed hardbacks. Her eyes drift over black-and-white photographs, vivid botanical illustrations, maps of ancient voyages. What began as an innocent enquiry has become more and more of a preoccupation. At first, she was aware only of an uneasiness in her stomach when wasting the morning in her flat or walking aimlessly around London. Now, a few months later, it has grown stronger, so that when she is not in the library, among these gilt-edged pages, a sense of loss, of uselessness closes in around her. It is not an obsession. It is not. Yet she recognises the anxiety of separation and wonders whether to mention it to her therapist. She can hardly explain the fixation to herself, let alone anyone else.

One book in particular captivates her: an early travelogue of Sri Lanka. She cannot fathom its hold on her, the thrill she experiences when turning its thick, weighty pages. Perhaps she has a natural deference for its age, for something that has endured over a hundred years. Or maybe it is how the book is revealing itself, *a slanting light sets ablaze the forest,* taking her through *dagabas,* the rock temple at *Polonnaruwa,* the gardens at *Muhumegha* and deep into the rainforest.

At its centre are four beautiful and strangely tactile photographs, their surfaces rich and velvety. With delicate half-tones and luminous highlights, the photographer has created an effect that is softly impressionistic, closer to the appearance of nature, of life itself. She leans in, fascinated.

*

One evening, a text from Anne arrives. She is out of town, spending time with family, suggests a walk on Hampstead Heath when she's back.

I'd love to, Stella replies.

Two weeks later, they meet near Highgate village. Anne is eager to start walking and sets off immediately along the foot-worn path with quick strides. The break from London has revitalised her, not just in energy, but appearance too. Her hair is shorter, though still long, its ends neatly cut.

How was your trip? Stella asks. Did you go home?

Anne nods. I need to get away sometimes. She turns and walks backwards to take in the Heath. I love it here though.

All around them, the trees are in spring blossom and dogs bound across the grass, weaving between runners and children on bikes.

She tells Stella how she never thought she'd stay in London after music college, couldn't get used to the grime, the noise, the exhaust fumes. She missed the moors and woods of her childhood, the solitude, but then she'd found the Heath. An unexpected wilderness in the city. She moved to a house-share nearby and has never lived far from it since, even when she had to cut back on heating, coffee and at one point, her phone, to afford the rent.

The sound of wind through the trees, she continues. Sometimes, I sit in the woods near my parents' house, and just listen. In strong winds, it's like a sea thundering overhead. That's what I miss most.

Stella thinks of the soft green fields behind her childhood home. The landscape was beautiful, but incapable of stirring the same depth of feeling.

How've you been? Anne asks. How's your dad? She pushes her hands deep in her pockets and gazes at Stella for a moment.

He's OK, thanks. He seems happier.

She nods thoughtfully. It's good he's getting on with his life.

A warm sensation rises up Stella's neck. She wants to say that it isn't, but knows that would sound rude. Sometimes, it feels like her mother was the only thing connecting her father to her, that although he loves her, he lacks the instinct to care for someone else. She feels selfish, self-pitying even, but can't help it. Her mother's absence, the lack of all she'd added to Stella's life, and perhaps most painfully the loss of a feminine space in which she'd felt safe and assured, makes her ache in a way that no one, and nothing, can soothe. She is thirty-one and has never felt more like a child. But she says nothing and they walk in silence for a while. Once or twice, she feels Anne looking at her.

I'm not sure Mum will ever get over losing my sister, Anne says, eventually. She's started hoarding. Not just my sister's things. I found boxes of chocolate past their sell-by-date, bundles of biros that don't work.

I'm sorry, Stella replies, quietly. Her words seem flimsy and inadequate. If anything, grief had pushed Stella in the opposite direction. In the early days of loss, she began to clear out more and more of her belongings, taking stuffed bags to charity shops, until her shelves and cupboards were empty and her apartment echoed.

Anne frowns gently. Sometimes, it doesn't feel real to be in the world when my sister's no longer here. She could be working in Leeds or forwarding me something funny on WhatsApp. Just knowing she was in the world made everything all right.

They reach the brow of the hill and look down at the vast skyline, the cranes, the multitude of buildings at various stages of being demolished and rebuilt as the capital renews itself, yet, just beyond, to the south, the land rises peaceably away from it.

Anne stares ahead, deep in thought. When I first came here, she says, I wanted to make the city feel smaller, kinder.

I had the idea – I think it was after a walk on the Heath – to leave little bunches of flowers for people to discover. I foraged on bike paths and in green spaces, left little floral offerings at bus stops and on benches. Flowers always remind me there are good things in the world.

Such optimism, Stella thinks, admiringly, and wishes she, too, could embrace this alluring way of seeing things. At that moment, Anne turns to face her and smiles. Close to, her skin is remarkably clear, unblemished by the city's pollution. A strange, timeless beauty, she could, in fact, be much older than she looks. Stella self-consciously raises her hand to her cheek to hide the bumpy rash there, a permanent mark from impetigo as a child.

Let's go this way, Anne says, gesturing away from the hill and towards a wooded part of the Heath. As they enter, the path quietens immediately. There is a large pond covered with algae and in the shaded light, its surface glows a rich green.

It's gorgeous here, Stella says.

All of a sudden, she feels completely at ease with this woman she hardly knows, who has some quality, some energy that carries her smoothly through life.

Do you mind if I ask what you do, Anne?

She inclines her head slightly. For a job? I teach the violin. To young children. Only part-time. I do what I can manage. Her dark eyes look almost apologetic.

I teach too. Well, I used to. Drama.

Not anymore?

She shakes her head, finding it unsettling to think of her former life. Too painful. She'd wanted to detach and move on, and her old friends had, in turn, lost interest after she didn't return their calls. This isolation had suited her for a while, but then a certain darkness had taken hold.

A lot of my friends from college perform, Anne says, but I prefer to teach. I go and watch them perform though. Like Gabriel, the friend you saw me with at St Martin's. We studied composition together for a year.

The breeze plays in Anne's hair and she tucks it behind her ear. I'm going to see him perform next week. You should come with me.

I'd love to, Stella says, feeling a surge of pleasure.

All of a sudden, they leave the woods behind. The entrance to the Heath comes back into view, the main road, the elegant cafes and shops of Highgate village. Above it all, the sky is still light and crystalline, the cold front keeping it clear. Together, they walk slowly back to the Underground.

Julia

Gerald is coming home, my love. Perhaps as soon as the end of the month. The letter Rose left for me was from your father and when I finally brought myself to open it, I found a blue envelope inside. I immediately recognised Gerald's left-sloping handwriting, the Ceylon stamp. He is leaving earlier than expected – some misunderstanding at the diplomatic office – and will bring your remaining possessions with him.

I feel as though I am recovering more of you. Not only the clothes, books, jewellery you took away with you, but perhaps something more: the items you collected in the last few months of your life. I imagine you visiting the local markets, the stalls laden with spices and candied fruit, and being tempted by the brightly coloured silks and other cloths for sale. The prospect of holding more of you in my arms fills me with a new vitality.

As you lay in bed in those first few days after coming home, I unpacked the few belongings from your case: your Kodak camera, a white silk blouse stained under the arms, some underwear, several empty, amber-coloured bottles. What were in these, my love? I tried to determine their scent – vaguely medicinal? – and tipped the bottles upside down. Only one yielded anything: a couple of reddish-brown drops, like rust water. You had so few possessions that I wanted to ask what had happened, why you'd left so suddenly, but made myself wait until you were able to talk.

From the beginning, you couldn't eat. Your weight had dropped so low, the doctor insisted you took in whatever nourishment you were able to stomach. I held a glass of milk for you, watching with dismay as you struggled to swallow. Through the open neck of your nightdress, I saw freckles on your skin, each ridge of your sternum painfully visible, a thin white strap line in your tan.

You asked me to leave the glass on the nightstand. I thought for the milk, but, no, your eyes were searching the clear surface for cracks and scratches. The imperfections. Mesmerised, you watched the light bounce off the glass in sharp flashes as the sun moved around the room. Your singular way of looking at the world around you, still there. Your green eyes still bright, brighter than ever against your bronzed skin.

Glass always fascinated you. I remember you photographing milk bottles, tumblers, large fluted pitchers, anything you could find in the kitchen. You piled them together or arranged them in a sequence, their fine cut detail glistening against a black background. I never understood the mysterious developing processes. Drawing with shadows, you called it. I see you now, leaning over the pantry's deep ceramic sink and mixing the chemicals with your bare hands. Like an alchemist. I warned you to be careful, but you wouldn't listen until acid seeped into a cut on your finger. Then you were more cautious, using gloves to prepare the emulsion and carry it away to expose the plates in darkness. There, you spent days experimenting on each negative, until you found a tonal range that pleased you. A peculiar, ghostly atmosphere, a combination of sharp focus and soft, recessive detail.

Where there had been frustration and tears when trying to capture life with a pencil, behind the lens you were more satisfied. Or perhaps the demands of the photographic process silenced whatever emotions were troubling you. No matter how hard things became, your desire to push through sadness or difficulty, to find knowledge in art or beauty, never left you.

Always that fierce drive to accomplish what you wanted.

One evening in late Spring, we were walking in Hyde Park and you told me about other female photographers who spent their lives working in obscurity, recording people in relaxed, natural settings. It was important to record those intimate moments, you believed, that would otherwise be missed or forgotten. You had your new pocket camera with you, in its leather carry case. You loved to use it outdoors in the early evening. The time of shadows and implication, you said. As we came to the edge of the Serpentine, the water was glowing in the setting sun, and for a moment my worries were silenced by the beauty of the scene. A large flock of Chinese geese was gathered on the path, staring at us as we passed. A pair of them entered the water. We were amused by the way their broad orange feet struck out behind them and I still remember the joy of laughing together.

A friend of mine's writing a book, you then said.

Oh, who's that?

Just someone I met at the Photographic Society.

Another photographer?

More a journalist really, though his pictures are very

good. He's travelling to Ceylon in a few weeks and has asked me to join him. I've always wanted to go.

To Ceylon? I must have looked shocked because you swallowed and turned towards the lake. That's so far away, I said, quietly.

Yes, far away, you echoed, and then turned back to face me. Don't try to stop me, Mother. I'll go anyway. You became flushed as you said this, and the corner of your mouth trembled a little.

I kept my face completely still. After a moment, in as smooth a voice as I could manage, I said that you must do what you thought was right.

You began to play absent-mindedly with a loose strand of hair, as you did when you were a child. You looked at me and I saw the little girl, whose hand had so often been in mine, gazing up at me for guidance. And then all of a sudden, something closed between us, and you raised the camera.

Let me take your picture, you said.

No! I tilted my face away, half-smiling half-grimacing, and feeling the start of a sick tremor in my stomach. Take it of the flowers, I said, gesturing behind you.

You shook your head, kept your lens fixed on me.

At that moment, a sudden rush of carriages passed

over the bridge, one after another, taking people out for the evening. You looked at your watch.

It's late, you said, putting your camera away and nodding towards the bridge where we always hailed a cab. As we were leaving, I turned for a final glimpse of the lake, but the light from the electric lamps was reflecting strangely in the water, and I had to shield my eyes from the crimson glare.

A few weeks after you left, I dreamt we were beside the Serpentine again, drifting along slowly, arm-in-arm in our usual way. The dream was so clear, I can still remember the tulips ruffling in the breeze, and the press of your arm, the warmth of your body. It seemed as real to me as any memory I have of that day.

It's extraordinary leafing through the book Diana sent me. I feel the intense heat of Ceylon, the fierce burning sun. Sometimes, I smooth my hand across the page and gently stroke the heavy cream paper as I read. I know it sounds strange, but I can sense you among the pages, just as I feel you in the heart-shaped pendant that hung around your neck and the scarf still scented with your perfume.

I see you walking out from the bungalow

towards the shore where a long unbroken wave is lifting, pausing, then crashing onto the sand. There are shells everywhere. Smooth pink ovals with rows of tiny serrated teeth. Glossy brown cones streaked with lines and dots, like music notes. You trace the markings on one with your finger, then lift it carefully from the sand and place it to your ear.

In your garden, I feel the scalding hot paving stones underfoot, the beating sun. White blossoms that were smooth and luscious in the early morning are now dry, their edges curled and yellow. You are lying in a hammock, sighing loudly in the way you used to when hot or bored, and looking at the leaves above. From time to time you drink from a glass of iced bergamot water. A little later, you hear the sound of mixing bowls from the kitchen, a conversation in Singhalese. Your housekeeper is preparing an evening meal and you go to help her, taking your camera with you.

I wake in the pitch black of my room, with the cotton pillowslip at my cheek, my body heavy on the mattress. I feel your loss acutely, my darling. I ache for you. Trying to silence my mind, I imagine a blank space for my thoughts to slip into, and wait for sleep. In the darkness, I see an image coming into focus, in greater and finer detail, until a single flower blossoms into the light.

Stella

Stella is dreaming of the book:

Five-petalled is the temple-flower. A creamy colour that deepens to rich yellow at its centre. The scent is thick and waxy-sweet. After the temple-flower are the palms, light and flimsy as torn cloud. Bushes are studded with blossoms of yellow and purple and crimson. The thickets are almost impenetrable: a tangled mass of green.

She is in the heart of the forest. A white track stretches ahead of her, a dark wall of green on either side. The air is hot, close, with a sweet fragrance. The path turns and she comes upon crumbling stone pillars, leaning at angles from a slope of grey rock. She walks between these pillars, bound with climbing plants and tangled thickets. There are crimson petals littered at the base of a tree, its bark gnarled and blistered with age. She continues along the path, winding through dense forest until the trees thin and suddenly the road vanishes from under her feet. She steps out of the ruins of *Thûparâma Dâgba,* straight into a bustling shopping centre behind the Angel Underground station.

Julia

When you were young, you used to hold your breath, as though you wanted to freeze yourself and the world around you. Later, in your photographs, you wanted to stretch time, to tell a story, to ask us to anticipate what happened before the click of the shutter and what came after. Now I see that your letters, like your photographs, raised more questions than they answered. Was this your intention, my darling? To leave me to make sense of your words and tell a story of my own creation?

I cannot look at the illustrations in the book. I know when I'm nearing one because they're printed on thicker card and stick out from the other pages. I flick straight past. In the centre is a set of photographic plates and I always close my eyes and turn them over without looking. It sounds strange, I know, but I don't want to see Ceylon through the author's pictures. I want to see it through your eyes, my love, through the photos you would have taken, the photos you took.

Last night, as I was trying to sleep, images flickered through my mind, all muddled and jumbled.

Your sister's eyes, extraordinarily large, with a deep sadness in them. My hand on the banister as I climbed the stairs to your room, the steps becoming steeper each day. The rain at the window. Drops sliding down the glass, joining another, then running on together. Louisa's face when I entered your room. A bundle of your letters tied with purple ribbon. And it occurred to me that we all freeze moments, whether we are aware of it or not.

*

The candles on the table are lit, the dinner places laid and the windows open to the warm evening. Louisa is talking about the guests she's invited, then places her hand on my wrist and tells me about the dish she's asked the cook to prepare. A French recipe of her grandmother's, with tarragon leaves and wine. I feel a wave of tenderness towards my friend, less irritated now by her fussing over these past few weeks. Even though I've felt constantly watched, I know she's only ever wanted to help, to console me. Perhaps I'm more tolerant knowing that I leave for London tomorrow. Back to the full tide of living. I'm travelling alone, despite Louisa's protests. I want to feel the gentle rocking of the train, to watch the

flashing green countryside, undisturbed. Besides,
I need time alone to think.

In London, a familiar life awaits, an existence
you once called stifling and limited. Our house in
Edwardes Square, the old mahogany chest in the
hallway for hats and coats, the faded crimson chairs
on the landing, your father and I sleeping side by
side every night. Yet what once held me now feels
empty and inadequate. Your loss has left a deep
hollowness behind.

Your father cannot talk about you. He becomes
irritated whenever I say your name, and retreats to
another room. He stays up late after I have gone to
bed, looking through his telescope at the constella-
tions above.

The silence is hard to live with, my darling,
and I do not have your love to comfort me. I have
always lacked a protective layer and experience life
in an intense, complicated way. I have never told
anyone this. Not your father, your sister, nor even
my closest friends. Whenever I saw you struggle,
I wanted to tell you about this deep sensitivity that
we share, but a stronger force, a maternal instinct
perhaps, silenced me. I feared making you worse,
as if to name it would make it more powerful.

You asked how I met your father, how we'd fallen in love and I wasn't honest in my reply. The truth is, I've never believed in love of the romantic kind. I think only one in a hundred people find the other half of themselves. I've never found mine. But the love I have for you is enough. A pure, more profound connection. I felt affection for your father, of course, and our life has progressed peaceably, for the most part.

And so my stay at this house will finish with a meal. Through the short nights and long summer days, these rooms have embraced me, murmuring with the hum of flies and the distant sound of the sea. I shall miss the view from this window: the lawn, the swaying purple globes of allium, the golden fields, the distant, luminous horizon.

Here they come – with the sound of laughter and the roar of a motor car pulling out of the drive – streaming along the path, in pastel-coloured evening dresses. I will smile and keep up the pretence. Louisa is kind to have organised this meal. I must let life in.

Stella

It is cold in his room. She fiddles with her cardigan sleeves, inhales and exhales deeply, before placing her hands on the table. She closes her eyes, then opens them again, asks him to remind her why they're doing this. Isn't what she's feeling just part of the grieving process? What's the point in going over the past again?

He leans back in his chair. Where do you feel your mother's loss?

She considers. I could be walking along Tottenham Court Road, and overhear someone speaking with their mother on the phone. Or in bed, when I'm unwell. She shrugs. Anywhere really.

I mean where do you feel it in your body?

Stella points to a place below her collar bone. Here, she says.

Remember that EMDR is about shifting how feelings are processed in the body. It will help with that, he says, gesturing towards the place her hand is touching. Her heart.

Everyone's response to grief is different, he continues, tidying the sheets of blank paper on the table, ready to start taking notes.

You cannot underestimate the impact of personal factors. Emotional regulation, coping mechanisms, prior history of trauma, access to support. I think we've already established that you found yourself isolated and alone.

His gaze drops to her hands on the table. I'm not blaming you, he adds, quickly.

His words remind her of something she once read: how emotional collapse can be hidden. That it must reach a certain stage before it breaks the surface and our carefully constructed identities fall apart.

Our work is to resolve earlier memories that have become stuck and still dominate. We've tackled some of the more recent episodes surrounding your mother's illness and death, the accident as a child, the bullying at school. Are you ready to look at another memory?

She pulls her cardigan sleeves over her wrists again, then decides to tell him about the white flower. That she cannot shake it from her mind. That while it doesn't belong to her past, it floods her with warmth every time she sees it, as though a long-forgotten part of herself is coming back to life. She doesn't know if she dreams of the flower or imagines it, or if she's now imagining that she has dreamt it.

It doesn't matter, he says. It made enough of an impression to appear in your imagination, so let's look at it.

She closes her eyes and places her hands on the table. He taps her hands softly with a pen, left right, left right. As she travels through time and darkness, images in her mind stretch and elongate. She sees glossy leaves unfurling, spreading against a concrete wall, then miniature white buds bursting into flower. There is a sweet fragrance. Jasmine? The blossoming image unreels and she hears the sound of cicadas, then senses a gentle presence nearby. She is drawn instinctively to it, yet the more she strains her mind to see it, the more it distorts. Frustrated, she can picture nothing more.

Some recesses of memory are easier to shed light on, he says matter-of-factly, as she opens her eyes.

His detached manner still makes her feel self-conscious. She wonders if he is like this with every client. At their first meeting, he'd shown enough compassion to gain her trust and since then, she has let her guard down and made herself vulnerable, but his manner has hardly changed. She finds their relationship strange, difficult to navigate. On her way out, he asks if she is lonely.

It is a sudden, surprising question.

No, she says, looking at him, and smiles.

*

The evening she sees Gabriel perform is unseasonably warm. Office workers mass outside the city's bars and restaurants. Empty buses sigh as they stop at traffic lights. The venue is a refurbished factory near London Bridge, constructed in the area's distinctive yellow brick. There's already a long queue outside by the time Anne arrives, smartly dressed, her long hair swept off her face in a chignon. Despite the sophisticated appearance, she seems more youthful than ever.

I can't wait to see this, she says, with childlike excitement.

In the dimmed light of the theatre, Stella can barely make out the audience seats or see Gabriel, though she can hear his soft piano playing. Obscured by darkness, the notes seem mysterious, strangely dislocated, and it is only now, as she reads the programme, that she realises he has composed the music for a play. How long since she has been in a theatre? Two years, maybe three, even longer since she herself performed. She imagines the bustle backstage: the anxious rehearsing of lines, the jittery anticipation.

She enjoys the production – it is an intimate, intense play with a small cast of four – but what captivates her is Gabriel's score, a surreal and eccentric sound that moves and merges with the unfolding action. The effect is unlike anything she has experienced before, and when the lights come up and the audience claps, she finds herself rising from her seat to applaud.

There is a cast party afterwards, in a nearby pub. Anne and Stella walk along the crowded pavements of Borough High Street, then through a succession of narrow alleyways until they reach Bermondsey Street. Once inside, she immediately recognises the cast members, standing in a group by the bar. Shortly afterwards, Gabriel arrives. He is dressed casually, with one cuff of his shirt loosely folded back, and his sandy hair worn in a tousled style. Anne takes Stella over to meet him.

Did you enjoy it? he asks, stooping under the low ceiling.

Yes. It was – she can't think of anything to say other than – great, and immediately regrets her choice of word.

He tilts his head, seems to consider her and smiles, but then stares into the distance. She shifts her weight from side to side, glances about awkwardly. After a moment, he looks back at her and runs a hand through his hair:

Sorry. I'm just tired.

She finds herself talking about the unpredictability of live performance, the forgotten lines, the stage directions that get messed up and scene changes that take too long. Oh, why is she still saying things? She feels herself blushing and glances down at the floor, but when she looks up, he is smiling at her. He folds an arm behind his head, starts to rub at his neck.

Um – so you're a friend of Anne's?

At that moment, she is given a drink by another cast member and pulled into their group. Everyone is friendly, welcoming.

Anne told me you used to act, someone says to her.

She nods, says nothing more.

As the city turns dark outside, she listens to their stories, their praise of Gabriel, of each other. They are a collective with the enduring bond of having performed together and she envies this sense of belonging.

Later, when she walks home alone, the roads are quiet, but the river is bustling. She idles beside it, watching the lights of passing boats gleam and shimmer on the water.

*

Anne's life is how, as a child, Stella had imagined her own life might be. Spending time with her is like opening a window in spring. Something light and fresh and long-awaited flows in, and as they drift around the capital together, Stella feels the faint stirrings of hope. During their walks, Anne talks about her childhood, the move from Toulouse, where she was born, to England at the age of five, and then her starting to learn the violin soon after that. The act of playing was all mixed up with the upheaval of moving, yet when she drew her bow across the strings, she was transported back to the family apartment in

France, its grey-blue walls, her grandmother's embrace. As years passed, the violin, once a source of comfort, became a punishing exercise, shaming even, with ever greater demands placed on her from music teachers, her mother, and finally herself.

One Sunday morning, near Regent's Canal, they come across a large scattering of petals across their path. An intense bloom of red. Anne stares for a moment, then looks up at the camellia bush in full bloom overhanging the pavement. She takes out a notebook from her pocket and makes a few notes, then smiles at Stella.

Julia

I call out your father's name as I close the door.
There is a musty smell in the hallway, the lingering
trace of roasted meat. On the breakfast room table,
an open newspaper. I gaze at the deep green velvet
curtains, half-drawn this morning, the mahogany
furniture standing in the shadows. Has it always
been like this? Our home resembles a painting by
that artist you liked. Sickert, was it? The same
gloomy palette. Darkness demands something of
us, you once said, though at the time I didn't
understand what you meant.

I feel tired, my love. Lack of sleep is catching up
with me and the darkness has a staleness to it, as if
holding the heat of several days together. I open the
French windows, let the fresh air in. The children
are playing next door, and I can hear their lively cries,
but in our garden, all is quiet and still. Shrubs and
plants droop with yellowing leaves. It is a few moments before I see him by the tree. He is reclining
in a chair, book on his stomach, an empty glass
beside him. As I walk over, he shifts a little, sits up.

You're back, he says, raising his eyebrows and smiling hesitantly.

Stella

Georgia O'Keeffe's white flower greets her every morning. She drinks her coffee beside it, drawn to the soft, tactile petals, the magnified leaves. She cannot help but stare into whiteness until the petals become folds of silk, linen and calico. Her mother is handling rolls of fabric, lifting and lowering each one carefully, like a sleeping baby. She repeats the name of the different shades: ivory, vanilla, almond, blush, accentuating the sounds, and glances down at her to see if her daughter is listening, but Stella cannot take her eyes from the mysterious cupboard behind. Only later, when she was tall enough to open the cupboard doors, would she discover what was inside: paintbrushes, canvases, embroidery threads, lace, naturally dyed ribbons, cardboard of all different colours and textures, porcelain doll parts not yet attached to make a body. Every item had potential in her mother's hands, for she'd learned to sew before she could use a knife and fork, and was still creating at the end of her life, measuring out her remaining weeks by the projects she could finish. Using her hands was the most natural way to calm and distract herself, to live.

Stella opens her eyes and looks again at O'Keeffe's

white flower, the soft, flesh-like petals curving inward towards a green heart. Even though she possesses neither her mother's patience nor her application, she imagines taking a paintbrush and making a start.

Her sleep is becoming heavier, as though medicated, her dreams more vivid. Fragments return throughout the day. Burning images, images that are brighter than the world around her. Dazzling white sand, a blue Persian plate, the mahogany piano inlaid with mother-of-pearl from her childhood home. Each one is like a painting that she cannot stop looking at, cannot stop thinking about long after seeing it. Together, they are as real as the delicate photographs in the library books she reads, weaving together with her memories in the vast tapestry of her unconscious.

*

Late afternoon. The window of her therapist's room is open to the warm summer air.

You're not into this today, are you?

She looks down. Sorry.

He shrugs. It doesn't matter to me. This is your time.

She shifts uncomfortably in her chair, lifts her long hair to cool her neck. He stares at her waiting for a response, but she says nothing and so he reaches down for his notes. The late sun is on the paintings behind him, and she likes the way it highlights bright patches of blue, amber, green.

Shall we start again? he says, handing her a sheet of paper.

She looks at the three circles she drew on it last time, the names neatly written in each one. A list of the people she can rely on for support. Nodding, she takes the pen he offers, taps it against her chin and wonders who to add next. He seems to relax now that she's engaged in a task and leans back in his chair, sipping his coffee. She can't help noticing the bluish skin under his eyes, the creases. As she draws another circle, she wonders what is causing his lack of sleep.

So, the memory from last week, the family holiday, has faded? he asks, after a moment.

No, not faded, she replies.

He looks down at her drawing with a strange kind of shyness. Have you thought any more about it?

She closes her eyes and remembers dazzling white sand, luminous waves swelling and lifting, the sound of splashing and the cries of other swimmers, her heart beating powerfully, all with the hazy confusion of a dream. She shakes her head. Irritated. By the pointless circles and his questions and the open window. Earlier, she thought someone was outside, listening to her and laughing. She realises she hasn't forgiven him for last time, when there were footsteps on the floor above and he'd seemed more interested in that other person than in their session.

She puts down the pen. Can we finish early?

He raises his eyebrows. Are you sure no feelings came up? No sensation in your body?

She doesn't tell him that the memory makes her feel light-headed and dizzy, that whenever she thinks of it, her entire body seems to pound with the force of her heart.

I'd like to finish now, she says.

*

She wakes suddenly with a feeling of panic, but can only remember an oval mirror with a gold frame. It had belonged to her mother or maybe her grandmother and though she believed it to have been discarded or lost, this long-vanished mirror reappeared in her apartment. She had stood on tiptoes to look into the glass, but there was no reflection, only a gold-rimmed blank.

In the bathroom, she freshens a sponge under the cold tap then presses it to her skin, frustrated by the lingering sense of unease. She tries to remember more of her dream, but there is only the mirror, its surface revealing nothing.

*

Early summer. The river shimmers in the sunlight. After a mild night, the air is already warm and full of vapour. She decides to walk east, past the houseboats, towards the new-builds of Rotherhithe and Surrey Quays. Her steps are purposeful and confident despite the negative thoughts in her head. Ridiculous and obsessive. Her therapist has suggested writing them down, but she is frightened of seeing the words. Too strange, too shameful, and so she resists and so they linger. She shakes her head in frustration, exhales, tries to slow her breathing, but quickly loses patience. She must maintain a routine. Teaching at least gave her that. And without it, she feels lost and adrift. She has attended interviews, circulated her C.V., shown interest in new opportunities, but has found no one willing to employ her. She regrets the years spent learning skills the city doesn't appear to need, and as if to highlight this, the path brings her directly opposite Canary Wharf. At that moment, sunlight breaks through the high clouds and its glass windows glitter. She turns her back, keeps moving.

Near Rotherhithe, where the tide is out, she finds the swans. They are nestling with a family of cygnets on the glistening mud. The sight of them lifts her briefly. It can be a good day, she resolves, forcing herself to brighten. It can.

Out of the corner of her eye, she sees a flicker of movement. Further along the path is an older woman, dressed in an elegant raincoat over slim-fitting dark trousers. She is bending down and looking into a patch of scrubland. Stella watches her gently part the long grass, as if searching for something, then stand up and with her face still averted, begin to walk away. As Stella watches her leave, she feels an unexpected wave of sadness, then an impulse to follow and, before she can stop herself, is slowly walking behind. For a few moments, she studies the bronze-brown hair, the petite figure, the slightly uneven gait, pausing a little on the left leg before lifting the right. Just as it all starts to feel utterly familiar and a warmth begins to swell in Stella's chest, the woman pauses and turns – but her face is entirely different from what Stella is longing to see. The woman smiles, briefly, then carries on walking until she disappears from view.

Alone again, Stella finds herself on a small peninsula of land surrounded by the river. Behind her, a building site is strewn with rubbish, broken bricks, a dumped sofa, yet here, in this forgotten part of the city, nature is flourishing. Tiny weeds blossom in the mud. She bends down to examine the miniature leaves, noticing the fragile veins running through them, the leaf's inner architecture, with an artist's eye.

Julia

One more day until Gerald visits. One more day.
I saw your sister yesterday. She took me in her arms,
pulled me close and I felt a fullness in her stomach.
A child in spring. I am excited, my love, of course
I am. A new life is something to celebrate. But I
cannot fully embrace the prospect of becoming a
grandparent. Not yet.

In town, the heat is unbearable and after your
sister's visit, I walked down to the river for some air.
There was little shade on the pavements and the sun
pounded my forehead. Everywhere was drowsy and
quiet. Blinds were drawn at every window. Only a
solitary market cart plodded along the empty streets,
the horse's head drooping on long reins; its echoing
hooves sounded almost mournful.

Beside the embankment, I stood in the shade of
the plane trees and touched the cool stone parapet.
As the Thames rushed past, I imagined you were
with me. I always feel you here, more powerfully
than anywhere else. I think of the times you took
me by the arm and wove me around slower walkers,
or pulled me closer to the river to watch a barge sail

past. We would imagine its journey along the final miles of the Thames as it curls back on itself before reaching the sea.

My memories of you in this city are overwhelming. Sometimes the air thickens at my elbow, shivers, and I feel your presence. I need only tilt my head with the smallest of movements to see you. Is it possible to go mad with longing? I fear that if I stay in London too long, I will go mad. A deeper loss is opening up inside me and I must find a way to blunt it for the outbreak of a visible madness is what I fear most.

Earlier, when I passed the chemist, I was tempted to enter and ask for a medicated draught to soothe me, but a fear of our family's darker compulsions persuaded me to keep walking. Yet how much longer before I collapse with exhaustion? Once I would have fought to grasp hold of something, but what I long to hold is the one thing I can no longer have.

I feel the weight of other people's judgment. They respect my grief, but cannot possibly share in it, for how can we know what it is like to be in another mind? To understand the degree of feeling that another must carry, tolerate, endure? The ferocity with which a mind is determined to follow its course, howsoever destructive.

Only when the intensity of feeling breaks the surface does our pain become visible in all its raw and ugly savagery.

We argued once, not far from here. I can't remember why, most likely something to do with your friends, but what I do recall is the shocked faces of passers-by. I was furious at you for involving me in a public outburst and unable to contain my temper, I shouted back and felt all the more embarrassed. For the rest of the day, I directed all the anger and shame I felt towards myself at you. I hope you forgave me for it. You see I was as afraid and ashamed, yes, ashamed, of your temper as I was of my own. But how I long to hear your voice now, even in public, screaming if you must, your face red with rage, if it meant you were still with me.

Stella

He knows that she loves France. She has told him about trips with her grandfather to the Rodin Museum in Paris, *le Jardin des Tuileries*, gazing up at Monet's vast shimmering water lilies. He always gives her coffee in the same mug with Monet's delicate twilight curved round its sides. She holds it in her hands before they begin, absent-mindedly stroking the printed colours with her thumbs.

Today she sees her mother's navy leather handbag, the one Stella carried home from the hospice. It held her mother's purse, a dental card for an appointment she would never attend, a cotton handkerchief with an embroidered blue flower, a glasses case in which Stella later found two passport photos of herself.

She tells him about the tears when she went through it all, having been persuaded by her father to discard and move on. And the pain when she discovered he'd thrown away her mother's makeup: the different eyeshadows, lipsticks, compressed powder that had touched her lips, her face.

Sunlight pours across the beige carpet, its pile soft under her hands and knees, her mother's back as she sits at the dressing table applying lotions from different bottles, back-combing her hair. Stella reaches up towards her and sees her mother's smiling face, reflected back, in triptych.

At the end, he seems pleased, asks what she has planned for the rest of the day. She shrugs her shoulders. On the way home she goes to a café and sits by the window for a long time with a coffee, staring out at a damp Fulham Road, her faint reflection superimposed on the glass.

*

The library is her refuge. A place to escape from the endless hours while she looks for work. Her financial situation is worse than ever. With no savings and no prospect of income, she is forced to break into a small inheritance from her mother, having already sold what personal items of value she owns: her sofa, bike, unworn clothes. She will not call her father. She will not. Even though she doesn't know how much longer she'll be able to afford therapy.

She has considered volunteering, but is surprised to find few opportunities within a commutable distance, and in her darker moments, a more self-defeating thought creeps in: no one will want her; even her free time, willingly given, would be unwelcome.

In the reading room, she opens the pages of her favourite book:

Our way diverges to the right, into a deep forest of gnarled trees. The leaves are silvery, slick with dew. The long wild grass is studded with flowers. In the undergrowth, palms bear coralline fruits of scarlet.

She reaches out a hand, can almost touch the red bead-like fruit, bright as jewels in the dim light. She is walking along a thin sandy track, the forest on either side thick with baobab and wild fig trees. Her footsteps scatter sand, fragments of leaves. Two white butterflies flutter across the thicket, land on a branch and then rise up and up, circling each other. Her body feels heavy – then an awareness of holding the book returns. The air is suddenly cool, and the reading room grows dark as rain begins to fall outside.

*

They'll only stop if you confront them.

He is looking at her intently, his words delivered in the usual manner, pared of all emotion, yet she's surprised to find herself reassured. He is right, of course. The thoughts she tries to avoid always linger, making her jiggle her foot distractedly when seated or pace around her apartment. Never one for confrontation, she prefers to turn and run. Once, she would have fled towards another for comfort and at the memory, she feels a patch of warmth flare near her heart.

And so they return to her past as he gently taps her hands, left right, left right. She must look dispassionately at what arises, as if watching a film or observing passing scenery from a train.

It's not easy. Memories that she'd forgotten resurface, some hitting her forcibly. Others seep into her consciousness, then gather more power as the day goes on, as her mind works on them. Strange that they have lodged in her memory at all. She is frustrated, angry even, feels their work in therapy is inflating things she'd rather not think about.

The other night, falling asleep, a memory of shouting at her mother jolted her awake. She was a teenager in the dream, her mother much older, trembling in the dark, her body emaciated by chemotherapy, an IV drip in her arm.

And then this morning, she was softly waking, lying on her back, when she had the sensation of being kissed, the warmth and press of a previous lover's body against hers. It was pleasurable, erotic, the heat lingering in her for some time afterwards. She cannot remember whether this actually happened, or whether it was a dream, her body desperate to be touched.

She has already told him about the episodes of rejection: a friend at school, a previous boyfriend, a group of students at drama college. Each one trivial, but plotting a course that brought her to an inevitable conclusion. The memories still hurt whenever she thought of them. He'd listened silently, appeared unmoved.

Do you feel better after getting that out? he'd asked.

She'd exhaled through an embarrassed laugh, waited for him to say more, but he simply got up to indicate the end of their session.

Today, she wants to talk about her father. She has remembered a time when, as a very small child, she'd been caught drawing all over his work papers and been subjected to his fierce temper. She ran to her mother for comfort, but was surprised to find her similarly censuring, a closed expression on her face. Those were rare moments, when her parents united against her. These days, her father is more approachable. The last time they spoke – on the phone a few months ago – he seemed reluctant for her to hang up, found ways to continue their conversation, his voice sounding more and more uncertain. It reminded her of a visit, last year, when she'd cooked for him. He'd watched her move about the kitchen, and as they sat together at the table afterwards, had patted her hand affectionately.

*

All of a sudden, it is summer. Trees have thick glossy canopies that overhang the streets and brush against the upper decks of buses. People wear flimsy, colourful clothes. There is bare flesh on the Tube, on the street, in the parks. Stella is slower to uncover, to discard layers. It is not only that her slight frame feels the cold. Every year, there's a certain shyness to overcome, but the rising temperature will eventually persuade her.

This morning, she leaves the Underground at an earlier stop and heads towards Holborn. Later she will go to the library, but for now she will just walk and enjoy the summer warmth on her face, the sense of her body moving after her therapy session. He is taking her back, time and again, to the beach. An episode he knows she hasn't resolved. A brief moment in her past, yet the more he leads her back through it, the more significance it assumes. Life does not usually provide the opportunity to unpick and refashion past experiences.

Increasingly restless, she is going for long runs by the river. Her mind and body demand it, as if trying to release some new, unfamiliar energy. She passes her next-door neighbour out running a few times. They swerve to opposite sides of the path, give each other plenty of space. Seeing him is no longer embarrassing, he is merely an annoyance, like the slamming of his door late at night, the occasional noise from the other side of the wall.

She runs farther and farther. Not just to outrun her thoughts, but to distract from the sensations in her body.

The nudge in her heart is now a constant ache, the fluttering in her stomach has settled into a ball of fear. She isn't sure whether it is a physical pain or some memory or emotion swirling around her body and sniping at her insides. All she knows is that yoga cannot relieve it. The stretching and lengthening used to bring about a release, but not anymore. The practise feels too passive, too gentle to dislodge the growing unease. She is shy entering the studio. In fact, any confined space makes her anxious.

Earlier, when her therapist had asked about her mother's art, she'd felt an opening in her abdomen. Not painful, not like a tear, more a sense of something unfolding. She had only felt this sensation once before, on the river path, at the sight of a solitary swan flying down the Thames, its long neck outstretched.

She reaches the crossing with Holborn Viaduct, pauses, then heads towards Russell Square. And it is there, among the multitude of white office shirts and summer dresses, that she sees him. His hair is greyer, his profile diminished a little, but the way he's holding himself, unmistakably him. When he sees her, he looks alarmed but they are too near to avoid one another and simply continue until, at a polite distance, they stop, and she meets his eyes. They exchange a few pleasantries and then he is striding away. She realises that she, too, has started walking, navigating the crowds with surprising speed.

At first, she sees the candle. She still has it somewhere. A blend of santal and poivre noir that evoked memories of their holidays. A hotel in Uzès, a fig tree outside their window, the taste of bitter coffee, bed sheets scented with dried lavender. The fragrance calms her in a way his voice used to. She had loved him because he was like her mother, gentle to be with, unworried by her, at least in the beginning. He was calm, patient, ready to listen. Yet he was unable to forgive. Memories keep returning to her over the coming weeks and shortly after she sees him, a strange summer sickness takes hold.

She is confused at first, her brain foggy as though lightly sedated. A day and night of low mood follows, which she dismisses as hormonal until she wakes with definite physical symptoms. Her head feels swollen, her eyes dry and heavy. She rises then has to lie down almost immediately to stop herself from being sick. The child-hood phobia of vomiting remains. She pulls the spare pillow over her face, hoping the cool weight of it will ease the pain in her head.

She hears people laughing and drinking in the bars and restaurants outside, dance music from party boats passing up and down the Thames, but the sounds are coming from another world entirely. Her bed and her body with its curious, new sensations become her only focus. In her darkened room, as the hours rush by hot and confused, she loses her sense of time. Her mind turns inwards. She has a fresh impression of her mother's suffering as her body failed, and the words Stella kept repeating to herself. Hold yourself together. Hold yourself together.

Unravelling. Endlessly unravelling. She sees the blue seat of an Underground train with a pattern of tiny London monuments in the moquette. She was obsessed with finding out who'd created the pattern. It was imperative, as if her mother's life might depend on it. Thinking about it gave her mind something to do as her body jolted on the Underground, the Tube carrying her to the hospital, to work, and finally carrying her without purpose when there was no purpose left.

And then, darkness. The river as grey as the clouds above it. Day after day, her first experience on waking was distress that her body was still breathing, her heart still beating despite her mind willing it to stop. The passing of time marked only by morning and evening trips to buy alcohol, not caring who heard the rattle of bottles, who saw her gaunt appearance, her face flushed with alcohol, who detected the rancid smell of vodka. Others couldn't watch her fragment, didn't want to be near it. The headmaster who dismissed her, the other teachers at school, the neighbours, even her father.

For hours, only these memories, nothing else.

The illness persists. Her body is exhausted, yet her mind races on. She cannot get comfortable. Her sheets are too smooth, too heavy. She takes off her pyjama bottoms and lies there naked from the waist. At some point, she manages to sleep, but her dreams are fearful, full of unremembered distress and she wakes with a thickly beating heart.

Other memories float out of the shadows. A different time. A different person. The cold of autumn in the air. They stood near the door after a tutorial and talked. There were group drinks. His gaze lingered on her. They talked again for hours, in soft, uncertain voices. They made love, his hands on her hips. His eyes half-open, gazing at her chest, her naked body.

He was the first to notice it. Her fear, her distrust of others. Not paranoia exactly, not then at least. You expect people to dislike you, Stella, you're looking for it. The uneasy expression in your eyes, always scanning around you.

She was surprised, thought she had hidden it all. She must act better. Layer up. But the effort of maintaining the performance was draining. He could sense the change in her, the briefer embraces, the lack of patience. She became unkind and self-absorbed. He decided to end it when they both knew it was what she wanted and afterwards there was no shortage of men who wanted to sleep with her. It was convenient, for she wanted neither a trusting intimacy nor a meaningful closeness with anyone. Other people's judgments don't matter if you don't care.

That night, she has a vivid dream that the river is surging towards her, rising and curling into a wave around her mattress, until a hoarse cry outside stirs her and enters her sleep. She sees a luminous moon hanging above the city, pouring its light onto the river and agitating the water birds. It merges with another moon, full, clear and cold above the hospice.

After the fourth or fifth day, she begins to scratch, raking her nails across her skin. She must have a rash, but when she lifts her t-shirt there are only the red abrasions of her own making. The itching continues and she scrapes furiously, tearing her skin. She takes anti-histamines with paracetamol, then any medication she can find, but relief is only temporary. Her nervous system feels permanently inflamed. Agitated, she rises, paces around her apartment, but exhaustion forces her back into bed. Ever more anxiety flares into her dreams, creating distressing searches for her mother, for unknown people, dreams in which she is endlessly running, and then a final, vivid dream. It is her grandmother's mirror, no longer blank, this time with a clear reflection.

Her mother. She is youthful, with glowing, bronzed skin, cradling a small child at her hip.

This is you darling, she is murmuring, pointing at their reflection. This is you.

The following day, the itchiness is milder. She gets up and dresses, no longer able to bear the solitude of her apartment, but at the lift, she feels faint and has to go back inside. That night, she has a pleasurable sensation of being tightly held and walking with another body pressed against her. On waking, she feels light and peaceful. The memory of this intense connection stays with her all day.

Several days later, she hears the intercom buzz. At first, she ignores it, assuming it is a courier for another flat, but it continues, longer, more insistent. Eventually, she pulls herself out of bed and looks at the small camera screen by the front door.

Anne.

Her first instinct is to step back, but then she picks up the phone.

H-hello?

Stella! Are you OK? You didn't answer my messages. I was worried about you.

Stella has not looked at her phone for over a week, cannot even remember where she left it.

I've been ill. Her voice is hoarse. She coughs, tries again. Some virus.

Can I come up?

Stella rubs at her temple, winces. Honestly, I'm fine.

It's number 44 isn't it? Anne asks, then disappears from view as she follows someone through the communal entrance. A few minutes later she is outside Stella's apartment, knocking softly on the door.

Just a minute! Stella calls out, hastily zipping up her jeans and fastening a bra under her t-shirt. She drags a hand through her hair, then opens the door.

Anne's face is concerned as she takes in Stella's appearance and peers behind her into the apartment. After a moment, her light frown lifts and she exhales quietly.

I'm glad you're OK. Do you mind if I come in?

Stella nods, stands back from the door.

Once inside, Anne hugs her immediately. There's a crush of paper and when they part, she is holding out a bunch of flowers.

Oh, wow! Thanks.

Stella flushes with pleasure, and for a moment, forgets her dishevelled state. Anne, standing in her apartment. All of a sudden, Stella is filled with an enormous sense of relief, and then inexplicably a deep longing.

Anne smiles, tilts her head. Do you think you can eat something?

Stella shrugs and Anne nods in understanding. She takes the front door keys, and returns a short while later with a bag of ingredients from the market nearby. For the next half an hour, Stella watches as Anne moves about the kitchen, washing the fish she bought, zesting the lemon, pleating the foil parcels. No one has cooked for Stella in this way for a long time. Halfway through, Anne takes off her bracelet and reties her hair. Everything she touches from her hair grips to the forks, the oven and even the scrubbing brush, receives the same considered attention. Stella finds herself unwrapping the flowers in a similar manner, taking time to cut their ends and arrange them carefully in a vase. She folds the brown paper and puts it to one side, unable to discard the packaging Anne has cradled in her arms.

Soon, the kitchen is filled with the smell of different flavours intensifying, of onions and other vegetables softening in the pan. A meal of white fish, ribbons of carrot and courgette, seasoned with garlic, lemon, thyme. The food is delicious, for it tastes of kindness, of friendship.

Afterwards, they remain at the table and Stella plays absent-mindedly with a fork. She is full, though not uncomfortably so, surprised at how quickly her appetite has returned.

You look better, Anne says, nodding.

Stella smiles, feeling shy all of a sudden. Now the meal is over, it feels strangely intimate to be sitting side by side with Anne, her table pushed up against the wall to save space in her small apartment. They are normally outside, surrounded by the swell of London. She shifts a little, conscious of her crumpled, barely out-of-bed state.

Thanks again for the flowers, she says, nodding at the vase and then before she can stop herself, begins to confide her growing fascination with botany, days spent in the British Library with ancient volumes in her hands, the vivid watercolour paintings and delicate black-and-white photographs. How the hours pass slowly like some kind of dream. She tells her everything while Anne listens without any sign of judgment.

When Stella finishes speaking, Anne looks closely at her, then says:

It seems to worry you, Stella, the way you spend your days – why?

I don't know. It feels strange. As though I'm a bit lost.

Anne smiles and shakes her head. That doesn't matter. I'm curious though. What is it you like about these books?

The flowers, I guess. She shrugs. Their beauty.

The truth is she cannot really explain, knowing only that the books and their delicate floral pictures go some way to filling the deep ache within. She closes her eyes and sees heart-shaped leaves, delicate curved petals, gold stamens. They have an ethereal beauty that makes her feel connected to something vast and complete.

I think I know what you mean, Anne, says. For me, it was music. It used to take me to this place. I can't really describe it. A place of consolation.

Not anymore?

It's different now.

There is a short silence.

After your sister died? Stella asks, quietly.

No. No. Anne says, picking up an empty glass and looking into it. Long before that. She sets the glass down. I don't really want to talk about it.

Of course, I'm sorry. I didn't mean –

It's fine. Anne smiles, then gets up and starts to clear away the plates. Stella follows her into the kitchen and together, they wash and dry the dishes. Every so often, Anne stops scrubbing and watches the precise order in which Stella is putting things away.

You could always work with flowers, she says, after a long pause.

Stella turns from the open cupboard to look at her.

You need a job, Anne continues. You love flowers. Why not work with them? Just an idea, she adds, but I could see you doing that. Really.

In truth, Stella has imagined working as a florist or even studying conservation, but to hear those words spoken aloud by another person somehow makes it seem possible. And, perhaps even more importantly, that she wouldn't be alone in trying.

Later, she stands at the window and watches Anne walk away. Their deepening connection is complicated. She's unsure what to do to, how to be, for fear of breaking it. There's something so familiar about Anne and discovering this kind of intimacy again is both pleasurable and intensely painful. Folding herself in her arms, she gazes down at the string of lights along the riverfront and allows herself to feel a quiet hope.

Julia

Half past two. If it were an hour later, I would get up, but I must put the book down and try to sleep. Its pages are becoming worn in places and faintly stained. My hands leave a permanent impression of my touch.

Stella

Her mother is not far away, in her bedroom, singing as she hangs freshly laundered clothes. A comforting smell of washing powder, the vinegary trace of glass cleaner. Stella senses her mother's presence long before she opens her eyes.

She is trying to take things gently after her illness. She makes herself lie in the bath and enjoy the warm water, the sensation of weightlessness. Afterwards, she takes time to massage cream into her body. She cooks herself proper meals, arranging the food on her plate with care as Anne did, before sitting down to eat in the long summer evenings.

Her first emotion on waking is no longer alarm and the horrible restlessness that previously made her rise and distract herself. There is, in fact, nothing. Only daylight pressing gently at her closed eyes.

She doesn't mention any of this to her therapist. It feels too intimate, too deeply internal, and besides, he seems more distant since her illness. He is quieter in their sessions, mostly leaning back in his chair and listening. Occasionally, he will pause when she finishes speaking, then launch into something unrelated to what she's just said. Today, he's taking her back through a memory in which she is holding her mother's hand, walking on a gusty beach.

Pale ridges of sand crunch underfoot. With each step, tiny pools of water form around her toes and ankles. They are looking for shells, for the small ivory-veined clams or tightly closed mussels found on the shore. She leaves her mother's side and runs to the water's edge, where she puts her hand in the seething foam. Ice cold penetrates her fingers and spreads up her arm. She turns to look at her mother, standing further up the beach, hair blowing in the wind. And in that moment, Stella is struck by a realisation: she and her mother are entirely separate. Her mother is distinct from her, with her own thoughts and feelings, and this feels both strange and completely natural.

She fast-forwards through their relationship, how she grew up, moved away, worked in another city and yet their closeness remained. Her mother, not needing to speak when they were together, not even needing to be physically present, just the fact of her being somewhere in the world was enough.

When Stella has finished talking, she avoids eye contact and glances around the room. His sitar has moved and is now leaning against the kitchen door. Has he been playing it since she last saw him? When she was ill, she'd concentrated hard on an image of his sitar, imagining its distinct sound, the comforting smell of old books in his lounge, hoping to feel his presence in her apartment. Has she always done this, conjured up another person by imagining the sounds and smells she associates with them?

He asks if anything has come to mind.

She takes a sip of coffee, tells him how she felt a nudge of happiness, once or twice in the week when remembering a joyful moment: getting her teaching qualifications, helping a student become more confident on stage, an apartment she rented by the sea one summer.

Your mind is simply returning to what it knows, he says, a touch dismissively. Trust in the new, he adds, and fixes her with such a meaningful stare that for a moment, she wonders if he can see into the future.

This is the closest he will come to giving her advice.

*

Anne's apartment is on the second floor of a Victorian terrace. She leads Stella through the communal area, past bikes and piles of takeaway fliers, up a short flight of stairs. Once inside, Stella's first impression is of softness. Everything seems layered and piled up. Throws of different textures and colours are draped over the sofa and chairs. On the walls hang vibrant paintings. Landscapes, a still life with red hellebores, a faceless woman seated beside an easel.

While Anne goes to the bathroom, Stella sits in the lounge and removes her shoes, placing them neatly on the floor. The room is crammed with mismatched furniture, books and photographs, the collected memorabilia of Anne's life, yet these are all carefully arranged so that the space feels homely and orderly. Stella thinks of the spare furnishings in her apartment, how the starkness is pleasing, calming even, yet she knows that it undeniably lacks warmth.

Anne smiles as she comes back into the room. Oh, you don't need to take those off! she says on seeing Stella's trainers. Sitting down, she follows her gaze to a photograph on the side table.

That's Meg, she says, nodding at it.

Stella leans closer. They have their arms around one another. The family resemblance is unmistakeable, the same dark hair and porcelain-clear skin, though Meg's face is fuller, wider, her expression more guarded.

She was my accomplice, Anne says. She always had my back. We were in our twenties then.

Anne leans back in her armchair and tucks her feet up under her long dark-green skirt.

Do you think it would have been easier if you'd had another sister? Stella asks, then immediately regrets her question.

Anne wrinkles her nose, gives a little shake of her head, though doesn't appear offended.

I don't think so, although perhaps I'd be less lonely sometimes. We shouldn't feel vulnerable when we're on our own, but of course we sometimes do. I think it's a primal thing, when we're on our own, don't you think? A sense of being unprotected?

Stella considers this, and nods, thinking of the constant tension between wanting to be alone and needing company, the ache of grief they both share. And although the pain hasn't left her, it is becoming more bearable, with moments of joy or, at least the memory of joy, nudging into her week.

After a few moments of silence, Anne reaches for her violin case. She moves over to the window with it and unlatches the clasps. Taking out the bow, she tightens the hair, pinching to test the tension, then applies rosin. Only then does she lift out the instrument. It is astonishingly beautiful, carved out of gleaming, copper-toned wood.

Anne sits in the alcove and begins to play. Slow, long, resonant notes. Her face is absorbed as she feels the long neck of the instrument and holds down the strings. Every so often her fingers quiver and the sound becomes more rapid and sorrowful. Mesmerised, Stella watches how Anne is transformed: she is gazing down, eyes half-closed, as though in this moment of intense concentration, she has found an effortless sense of peace.

Stella feels a gentle tightening at her temples. The music seems to move through her, forwards and backwards simultaneously. It is the first time she improvised on stage in front of an audience, under a beam of light, exposed and vulnerable. It is the sound of her mother singing, her voice untrained, yet pure and true to pitch. And it is the deep sensation in Stella's heart, of being pulled towards another and encouraged to trust.

Suddenly Anne stops playing and lowers her arm. She smiles to hide the sadness that has come into her expression, distractedly taps the pads of her fingers.

My hard skin is coming back, she says, and explains how as a teenager, her fingers had developed thick callouses which sometimes became sore and inflamed.

They talk for a while longer before Stella leaves Anne half-heartedly practicing some phrasing, with her violin lowered. Outside, on the tree-lined street, Stella turns and looks up at the window. Anne is no longer sitting in the alcove and the room is dark, but in the coming weeks, whenever Stella thinks of that room, it is always sunlit.

*

Rain falls silently outside the British Library. Inside, Stella is reading:

Beneath a tall, red-brick gateway you pass into the sanctuary of the Bo-tree, guarded on all sides by a high wall, covered in ferns and glossy-leaved creepers. In the centre, the holy tree rises above its offspring: innumerable ancient seedlings that are now magnificent specimens. Together, they create a forest of shade. In the calm twilight, the scent of champaca flowers offered by worshippers lingers in the air.

There are some brownish fingerprints on the page and deep indentations in the paper, as though someone has held the book tightly. Was it her? She hadn't noticed the marks before and tries to brush them away with the back of her hand before giving up and turning the page.

At first, she sees a solitary white flower in soft focus. Then as her eyes take in the image, she hears a female voice, frustration in her tone. It is too dark, she is saying, the camera lens cannot separate shadow from light. She is raising and lowering the point of view, searching for proportion, foreground to background. Only one photographic plate remains, this much is clear, only one plate of all the plates she carried with her.

High above, a breeze stirs the holy tree's thick canopy, lifting a branch, and then suddenly, light illuminates the precinct. It burnishes the tilt of a petal, the curved tip of a leaf, and the shutter falls.

In the silence of the library, all Stella can hear is her heart beating.

Julia

Gerald, deeply tanned, sits before me. Smiling and cheerful, he is much the same as ever, though perhaps his manner is a little forced and there's an edginess in his voice. While he's talking, my gaze drifts to the two large cases inscribed with your initials, in the hall, one with the faint markings of SS Mantua, the passage you took. I imagine your photographic plates inside, safely packed in negative boxes, your books, clothes, perhaps a glass perfume bottle with the remains of your favourite scent.

It's strange, he's saying. I always picture rain when thinking of London. I wasn't expecting this heat! He gestures towards the window, the deep blue sky overhead.

I smile politely. When are you going back?

He pauses, begins scratching at his arm. I'm not.

Oh. I thought – I break off, puzzled. Your mother told me about a promotion, that you were doing so well.

He shakes his head. I'm not going back. There is a strained silence while he looks down at the floor, then exhales quietly.

Not knowing what to say, I shift a little on the sofa, and find myself looking once more at your cases in the hall.

Well, thank you for bringing her belongings home, Gerald, I say after a long pause.

It's the least I could do. His face softens and as he leans forwards in his chair, he looks at me with such sadness that I can hardly bear it.

I'm so sorry, Aunt.

I nod, silently, then swallow. Is that everything?

Yes. More or less. Everything that matters.

I'm uneasy hearing this. What does he mean? I can't bear the idea that he has left anything behind, however small or worthless, even the old enamel comb you used in your hair. Anything that still holds a trace of you.

He sits back in his chair. I assume the doctor said – Yes. I interrupt, feeling my hands start to shake. Typhoid, most likely.

He nods thoughtfully: She had been travelling around the country. To the interior. Unfortunately, it was just after the rains, when the flies come.

My mind is full of questions, but I shake my head and look down. I imagine clouds of black flies swarming over your food and crawling on the mosquito net above your sleeping body. Then I see your bare leg, casually thrown out of the sheets, exposed and vulnerable.

But why make the long journey back if she was ill? I say, eventually. That's what I don't understand.

He reflects for a moment. I'm not sure she would have known anything was seriously wrong. Not at first. These tropical illnesses can come on slowly, with a headache or overwhelming tiredness. There is, of course, a chance she caught it on the boat home. Though that is less likely, he adds, quietly.

Tears form in my eyes and he looks away while I wipe them. I ask him to tell me anything he knows about your last months. I am jealously possessive of any information about you; I want to remember it all, as if I had been there with you. As he talks, I try to capture what he says in a series of images, concentrating hard to create memories like photo-graphs. I imprint on my mind the hundreds of fireflies, glittering like stars, that you saw. The temple near to your cottage where he found you staring at the intertwined branches of a tamarind tree. The flawless blue sky, the surprisingly cool air at dawn that you compared to a wintry English sunrise. I try to intensify the moment – by summoning the same

joy, surprise, or amazement you might have felt –
to better commit the images to memory.

You had little interest in Colombo's colonial clubs
and hotels, with their claustrophobic, judgmental
interiors. You would take a cart in the cool of the
evening to a quiet garden about five miles from the
cottage. Here you would sit among the palmyra trees
or stroll through the lush green vegetation, always
with a camera over your shoulder.

You were deeply interested in the local people,
in capturing them with your photography. You
sought out momentary encounters amidst the rush
of life. A passing smile between a young mother
and her son as they wrap bundles of food in cloths.
A frenzied scene on market day as traders carry
baskets of apricots, dates and almonds.

Your work was admired in a studio on Galle Street.
You never told me about a studio, but as the months
passed, your letters became increasingly secretive and
suggested disturbing emotions I couldn't recognise.

You visited the interior of the island to assist
your writer friend.

Describe it for me, Gerald, I ask.

His expression changes, then he says:

You enter a profound silence. A different kind of

light. The air is incredibly pure and after the rains, it fills with the scent of jasmine and champaca. Vegetation is thick, impenetrable, except where the sun breaks through. The beauty of it is extraordinary and you stumble upon dazzling sights, like a Sāmbhar deer, silhouetted against the mountains, or a vast, glimmering lake. But the longer you are there, particularly if you're alone, the more you can feel isolated, vulnerable, easily lost.

He sometimes wondered whether he could have immersed himself in one of those remote areas, whether a part of him could have got used to that life, far from the politics of his department and the outdated attitude of his superiors. He might have helped improve irrigation to the villages or perhaps taught in a local school. To offer some meaningful help. In the last few months before leaving Ceylon, he'd received anonymous letters, all in the same handwriting, informing him of bribery and acts of brutality in his department. He never found out who sent them.

He sits back in his chair for a moment, deep in thought, and then turns to his final memory of you.

The last time he saw you was a few nights before you left for the interior. He was bringing a book to your cottage and you were sitting outside with your friend from the studio, Grace. He hadn't met her before. You had seemed tired, he thought, subdued. In the light of the spirit lamp, he recalls seeing shadows under your eyes.

She'd lost weight, aunt. It's true. But she was the same Helena. As far as I could tell, he adds, in a low voice.

When he'd returned to collect your belongings a few weeks ago, your housekeeper, Rama, was upset. She shook her head, kept gesticulating outside. In halting English, she told him that she'd been worried about you. At first, she thought it was dehydration causing your stomach pains, your loss of appetite, that your body had never adjusted to the heat, but then after several weeks you stopped having meals at the cottage, only sipping a little pomegranate juice after returning from the studio late in the day. Once she heard you vomiting and she made you tea from boiled Lunuwila leaves, an old Tamil remedy for sickness.

A twist of jealousy makes me inhale sharply, then the memory of your first night back at home returns. The image of you, head over the toilet bowl, hands resting on the white porcelain rim, and your coughing – the hoarse, unrelenting coughing – then a retching that still haunts me. Every time, the sound was a series of fine cuts to the inside of my arm.

She often struggled with her stomach, I say distractedly.

I don't think you understand, Aunt, Gerald says, leaning forwards in his chair.

I don't?

He starts to say something more, then stops, seems to change his mind. The room is getting uncomfortably warm and I go to open the window, pausing with my hand on the sill. Forgive me, my darling, but I have to ask him. I have to know.

Was she – taking something, Gerald?

I hear him sigh.

I don't know for certain, Aunt – but a lot of people are.

When I turn to face him, he looks at me, almost pitifully, then springs up from his chair.

Here, let me help. He comes beside me and raises the sash window with a firm push. We both stand there for a few moments in the fresh air. The sky is still blue but now streaked with gold clouds in the upper atmosphere. It must be early evening. Your favourite light, my darling.

I sense Gerald turning towards me, but I don't need to hear any more. I ask him to carry your cases upstairs. After he has heaved each one into your room, we gaze around it in silence. Your pale curtains are half-drawn. The light is soft, dim shadows spreading. I pick up a photograph from a nearby table and hold it out to him.

When she was seven, I say.

He takes the picture and glances at it, then hands it back silently. I set it down among the other portraits of you. There is a fine layer of dust covering the table and my heart softens when I notice another set of fingerprints in it that can only be your father's.

We both linger in our own thoughts for a few moments until Gerald excuses himself for an engagement and I follow him downstairs. Collecting his hat from the sitting room, he pauses by the book on the side table, angles his head to read the spine.

Ah, so he did get it published, he says, opening the cover and flicking through the opening pages.

Who?

William. He glances up at me and frowns at my puzzled expression. The writer Helena travelled with. Did you not know?

I shake my head, embarrassed.

Nice fellow. He closes the book and gently pats the cover for a moment.

Well, look after yourself, Aunt, he says, his face brightening as he comes to kiss me, then walks out and into the evening.

Stella

In the following weeks, the temperature in the city builds. Early one morning, she wakes to find the air unusually humid, promising a sweltering day. Brushing her hair in front of the mirror, she attempts to tie it in a bun, but it slides out messily so she leaves it loose around her shoulders. At the back of her wardrobe, she finds a white camisole top, enjoys the smooth fall of silk as it slips over her chest, her abdomen, falling at her hips. She steps into a long skirt with a floral pattern and surveys herself in the mirror, then reaches for a brown leather belt which she fastens tightly at her waist. The outfit is considered, feminine, sensual even, and she finds herself smiling at her reflection in the mirror.

Outside, the river shimmers the palest of blues. She closes her eyes and inhales deeply, enjoying the warm air on her face. For a moment, she could be by the Mediterranean. When she opens her eyes, everything is glittering: the water, the silver skyscrapers, the gilt edgings on Tower Bridge. On rare days such as these, London is lifted to an ethereal beauty.

Once she heads away from the river, the heat becomes stifling, and the air is heavy with the smell of fast food from street vendors. There is a waft of sewers near the Underground. She finds Anne waiting for her, just outside the entrance, studying a small plaque in the stone wall. Like Stella, she's dressed for the heat, in a long, flowing black dress. Its vintage style makes her look older, or perhaps it is the way the bright summer light is picking out silver strands in her hair.

It was Anne who'd suggested they visit the houseboats by Tower Bridge on the weekend they open to the public. They're right near you! You'll love them, she'd urged. Ever since moving to this part of London, Stella had gazed at the houseboats, drawn to the romance of living on the water, the protective sense of community. From a distance, their world had seemed compact and self-contained, as timeless as the river flowing beneath them, yet upon entering the mooring – through a narrow archway between the wharves – the perspective shifts entirely. There is a welcoming string of lights along the pontoon and what had appeared to be low bushes and shrubs from the river path are, in fact, tall trees growing on rafts. One barge is given over to bikes, another to recycling bins. Stepping onto the first boat, she anticipates a lurch, but finds the deck stable and walks steadily along it. At the end, a young man with curly black hair, wearing a pink t-shirt and espadrilles, takes a small fee and gives them two maps.

They begin to explore the outermost boats first, an assortment of Dutch and Thames Lighter barges converted into homes. Walking along the decks, glancing down into windows, Stella catches sight of a neatly made bed, a polished wooden table, piles of books, a laptop, the intricacies of lives rarely observed other than by passing boats. It is oddly intrusive to glimpse other people's lives like this and yet she finds herself compelled to look.

Anne has discarded the map, lets herself be steered by whatever draws her. In fact, only a group of grey-haired women seem to be reading the guide. Most visitors are exploring at random. As they walk and jump between the boats, Stella feels their footsteps vibrate through her. Every so often there, there is a faint whistling as the breeze passes through the rigging.

After a short time, they reach a raft in the centre of the houseboats. An enormous quantity of flowering shrubs and tall trees are growing, so many that barely a patch of earth is visible. Ferns sprout alongside daisies, wild geraniums, honeywort, foxgloves, violets, all carefully planted to create a woodland effect.

Glancing around, Stella is suddenly dizzy and has to lean against a rail to steady herself. Perhaps it is the constantly moving decks or perhaps she is disoriented from looking up at the trees. Anne is happy to wait, watching the gardens rise and fall in the wake of passing boats.

How do they grow so tall here? Stella thinks out loud. Their roots can only be shallow, she adds, glancing up at the treetops then quickly looking down.

Anne follows her gaze. I was wondering that, too. It's incredible.

My mother would have loved this, Stella says, quietly.

Leaves of every shade of green, fluttering outside the window of her mother's studio. Captured in paint, thread or paper. Stella can almost smell the fabric and hear the wind blowing through the leaves, senses mingling. Soft green branches reaching in through the studio window, leaves unfurling, as if trying to touch the creations within. For their garden had been an extension of her mother's art, tended loosely, lovingly, with the same attention and patience. Later, Stella had worn her mother's red anorak, used her secateurs and picked flowers from her garden, taken them to her in the hospice. One of the final acts of love, echoing the many times her mother had left snowdrops or bluebells in her room. That day Stella had rested her head on the stiff sheet of the hospice bed, felt her mother's hand stroke her hair, and wanted to stay a child forever.

Do you ever dream about her? Anne asks, softly.

Sometimes. It's more an awareness of her really, just

before waking. As though she's been with me all through the night.

The brutal memories of the hospital, her mother's emaciation, the body's violent response that followed her starvation, horrifying images that would burst into Stella's mind at night and wake her, are rare these days. Dreams of her mother are lighter now, almost graceful, with a sense that she has moved on, rather than faded away.

And you? Do you dream of your sister?

Anne nods. All the time. I think she's trying to remind me she's still there.

Can I ask you something?

Sure.

Why did you stop performing? You seem to have had such a passion for it.

She sighs, squints into the sun. Something happened, New Year's Eve many years ago. A car accident.

She was physically unharmed, but not unaltered. Afterwards she would get a sharp pain that spread across her chest whenever she walked into confined spaces or the darkness of a concert hall. She began to dread going into college, and although she passed her degree, she knew she'd never have a career as a performer.

At some point I stopped fighting, she says, tucking a strand of hair behind her ear. I've got past it now, though my mother has never forgiven me. She rolls her eyes and smiles. Occasionally I do wonder if I'd held on and endured the discomfort, whether I could perhaps have pushed through. She reflects for a moment, then brightens. I'm determined to live with less caution now, not more.

Yes, Stella says, me too. Far from sharing Anne's regret, she finds herself admiring her friend even more. Not just for her honesty, but for placing self-preservation above everyone's expectations of her. Sometimes, it requires more courage to stop what we are doing, pause, take stock, than to force ourselves on.

They lean out over the smoothly flowing river, placing their elbows on the rail. The sun is still warm and the pleasure of it on Stella's skin, the way the light is catching on the water, the gentle movement of the boat, and perhaps something else, something impossible to determine, all produce a deep sense of contentment in her.

Just before they leave, Stella crouches near the violets and takes out her phone. The pendant from her necklace swings out as she leans forwards to photograph the delicate mauve petals and bright green leaves, thriving here in spite of the wind and salt air.

Julia

Colombo, 8 July 1909

Dearest Mother,

*Forgive me for not writing sooner – I've been making
preparations for a trip to the interior with William.
He wants to include my photographs in his book. As
you know, I prefer to photograph people, the rush of life,
but I've been practising still life in a garden nearby.
I'm trying to capture the fading beauty of flowers, to
give the images movement, a sense of unfolding,
unfurling, perhaps bursting out of a dark background.
I'm still undecided. I've made some friends at a
photography studio in Colombo. They think my photographs are quite good! At the beginning, they couldn't
believe they were taken by me –*

Colombo, 12 August 1909

Dearest W,

*What do you think of the photograph on this postcard?
It is one of mine! A cattleya triane we found on the
mountain path to the Bo-Tree.*

*I leave tomorrow for home. The idea exhausts me
already. London is my past. Here, I'm journeying
towards something. I'll write soon.*

With love, yours,

H x

Stella

White, pure white. A flowing fabric, delicate, sheer, swelling in the breeze. There is fresh air. Bright sunlight. A flash of green across windows. Follow the leaves and you will find her for she is there, humming quietly, creating with her hands, while the white curtain is rising, floating, billowing in the breeze.

Julia

I have been through it all now. Your clothes,
carefully folded – by Rama? – in a delicate paper
I've never seen before, intricately flecked with tiny
chips of wood and threads. A blue shawl in lustrous
silk with the initial W hand-sewn into the corner,
a rustic linen blouse that you never had a chance to
wear. The photograph of me that you took beside
the Serpentine just before you left. My face caught
in that uncertain expression. The background is
dark, slightly blurred, placing me in a strange sort
of isolation. You had written on the back: *Aletheia*.
Truth. Those words again. Knowing you had this
image of me with you touches me deeply. There is a
box of photographic plates, tied with purple ribbon.
Did you develop these? I cannot find the prints.
Perhaps the studio in Colombo has them. And your
correspondence: the unfinished note to me, the
postcard you never sent to William. After holding
them, I cup my hands to my face, inhale deeply,
detecting the faintest touch of your scent.

There are many angles from which to view a
subject, you once told me. Each one conveys its own

version of the truth and, like one of your carefully composed photographs, you showed me only what you wanted me to see. A partial view, leaving me to determine the truth, the reality, or to construct one for myself.

I see you now, legs crossed, sitting on the bench outside your cottage. Your hair is tied up, legs naked under your dress, bare feet. You are smoking, listening to the rhythmic sound of water lapping on the shore. A cool shower has refreshed you after your long, dusty trip to the interior. There is food in miniature glazed dishes on the table, slices of jackfruit, a coconut chutney prepared by Rama. You look happy, my love, as you gaze at the sunset. You are waiting for the sun to turn the water a delicate pink, as it does every evening, just before it drops below the horizon. Is this my act of creation? So be it then, for this is how I choose to compose your picture.

You recreated yourself by going away. I can see that now. Travel seemed to unlock something in you, to allow you to abandon your old self and begin to construct someone new. Perhaps you discovered a world as bright and luminous as the Japanese prints on your bedroom wall. I gaze at them sometimes and wonder. How little I understood when you left.

I, who had lived so carefully, so narrowly. You were always inquisitive, always inclined toward the unknown, ready to explore and embrace new experiences. What made you so courageous?

Diana is sustained by her faith. It shapes her life and gives her something to grasp onto. As we took it in turns to sit beside your bed, she was remarkably calm, and in the aftermath of your death, she became calmer still. She felt closer to you, had no inclination to revisit the sequence of events, never wished for a different outcome. But I cannot accept the predetermined flow of life. I wrestle against it and believe it is all a terrible game of chance. How else to explain why you were taken from me?

In my darker moments, I feared your sensitivity had overwhelmed you, that I had failed to give you the tools you needed to withstand this part of you. Yet, in the end, it was your physical frailty that betrayed you. You had neglected your health so your body was vulnerable, but you made it home. Somehow you made it home to me. Did you know how little time there was left? It bothered me when Gerald talked of you not eating. I wish I had asked if he knew more, but there's little point in going over it all now.

I have started to see a particular image of you when I close my eyes. I often dream of it too:

You are walking in a garden, camera slung over your shoulder. Head slightly bent. You're going from shrub to shrub, looking closely at the leaves. I imagine your thoughts, determining the best angle and the compositional style. When you see me, you smile and hold out your hand.

Stella

He is tapping her hands more tentatively now, more slowly, then stops. She hears him sit back in his chair as he starts to talk her back through her childhood holiday. The late-night arrival in another country, the air still humid, waking the next morning in an unfamiliar room. At first, she sees a series of images, like photographs hanging on a string. A burning sun. Green pine trees above a large, shockingly blue swimming pool. The long beach with dazzlingly white sand. Her mother reading on a sun-lounger, wearing a floral sarong tied at the neck. Memories, sensations in her body begin to form behind the pictures. The pleasure of eating buttery sponge cake in the afternoons. A day trip with her parents, restless and fidgety while being driven along dusty roads. She frowns slightly, gives a little shake of her head.

Picture yourself on the beach, he says.

She sees the winding path through pines that leads to the sea, feels a carpet of needles underfoot and then sand which hardens near the water's edge. Tall green waves, twice her height, break with giant crashes of spray. She can hear the distant cries of swimmers, has a sudden desire to be with them, beyond the outer line of waves. In the shallows, the seething water pummels her calves and her heart begins to race. She stumbles, half-falls, staggers on. The waves are thundering and she tries to sense their rhythm, to count the pauses between them, but suddenly a wave is rising directly before her and instinctively she throws herself into it. Then she is plummeting, being spun round and round, over and over, in the raging water. She tries to surface but is drawn up into another crashing wave which plunges her back under. She is falling again now, deeper and deeper, until she lands on the sandy floor. As she experiences this spiralling descent all over again, as she is lying there, it all unfolds with the time-lessness of a dream, so that it seems she is endlessly gazing up at the dark clouds of churning water, to a white blaze of light.

When she resurfaces, she gasps for air, her body heaving and shuddering, then fear sets in again, almost immediately. A wave is about to break before her and she swims as hard as she can, propelled by its energy, towards the shore. As soon as she is able, she puts down her feet and half-runs, half-stumbles from the water. She flings herself onto the sand, lying face up, coughing between gasps, the air making a strange, wheezing sound in her throat. Her heart still pounds in her chest.

As her breathing slows, she opens her eyes and meets his gaze. He is looking directly at her. There is a new expression in his face, almost vulnerable. He slowly gets to his feet, rearranges his papers on the table and clears his throat to signal the end of their session. She shifts herself out of the chair and unplugs her phone from where she left it charging.

It is only now, as she glimpses his books on the shelves that she sees the study of her childhood home, the cabinet of her mother's hardback books. They were in fact her grandmother's, with her name, Ivy, written inside them. Long works spread across two or three volumes, bound in black, burgundy or red leather. From time to time, her mother would carefully lift one down for Stella to read. The stories were varied, illustrated with images on thick cardboard plates, but the real treasure was tucked inside. Tiny brownish flowers pressed between blotting paper. A trace of her mother's mother in the fragile remains. She remembers the smell of the leather and the sweet almond-like fragrance of old paper.

On leaving, she sees a woman at the far end of the alleyway. Her hair is long and falls in blonde waves which sway around her shoulders as she walks. The potted plants have grown in the past weeks and now overhang the path, so Stella has to pause to allow the woman to pass. She is young, early twenties, fashionably dressed in loose fitting denim jeans, white trainers, a T-shirt. Her frame is thin and her breastbone pronounced, she fiddles nervously with a delicate gold chain around her neck. In their exchange of looks and polite smiles, Stella senses her apprehension, notices an expression of faint alarm in her eyes. At the end of the alleyway, Stella hears her therapist's door open, and she turns to see him welcome the woman inside. She keeps walking.

Julia

Last night, I finished your bedspread. I put
the final stitches in the floral motif at the centre.
A circle of lilies, white as the flowers on your coffin.
The silk fabric brushed against my skin as I carried
the cover upstairs and laid it over your bed as though
covering your sleeping body. It was you who showed
me that making things, even in obscurity, matters,
for the traces of a life remain within the created object. How much more respectfully do we treat these
precious items? How gently do I hold your photographs, how carefully do I protect the glass plates
etched with their image? You are in them, my darling.

Tomorrow, I will visit a darkroom in Flood Street.
Apparently, there is a network of these rooms all
over London to assist the travelling photographer
and support the novice enthusiast. Did you know
that, my love? I am looking forward to mixing the
developing fluid, as I once watched you do, carefully laying one of your photographic plates in the
tray, sensitive surface upwards, then pouring the
chemical over it, and rocking the plate with little
movements to ensure an even flow. I'll be more

comfortable doing this with the guidance of others.
I have much to learn and little practice of a skill
which I think experience alone can teach.

It is hard to say how long I've been standing here
at your bedroom window, but the house opposite
is now brightly lit, and the sound of a piano comes
from the tall open windows. There are dark silhou-
ettes inside, voices chattering, the occasional burst of
laughter. The world feels alive this evening.

So, you knew him, my darling. You knew the
author of the book I am holding now. The hand
who wrote this guide to the ancient civilisations,
the landscape, all that Lanka has to offer the travel-
ler. I close my eyes for a moment, touch the green
fabric covering the book, knowing every nuance
and slub in the weave. Feeling my way to the thick
card of the photographic plates, I take a deep
breath and open my eyes.

Stella

A hot summer's evening. People sit in large groups on the grass by Tower Bridge, talking and laughing, while overhead a gentle breeze sifts through the plane trees. Sometimes a single word or laugh is audible, followed by an eruption of sound. It is late, but the sun is only just setting, casting a pale gold light on the Thames.

Tomorrow, she has a job interview – an independent charity looking for conservation workers to catalogue the native plants across a vast site of grassland and woods. It is the first job she has actually wanted. But tonight, Stella is not thinking of the future. She is enjoying this evening as she walks home. These moments of pleasure are more and more frequent now, sometimes joining together in a stretch of happiness.

The path leads along the river. She stands still for a moment, takes in the wide expanse of sky above London, clear and blue. The light is dazzling, preternatural, as if she is under the light of another continent entirely. She can almost see mountains in the sky, vast clouds, innumerable stars above a distant ocean, and a sense of something there, just beyond. Still gazing up at the sky, she begins walking slowly again, but in a few strides, she is back in her familiar landscape, with the packed bars and restaurants, the string of lights looped between lampposts, vast historic anchors exhibited along the riverfront. There is a burst of laughter from above, the loud hum of conversation. All the windows of the apartment blocks are open, people are socialising or sitting out on their balconies. A sense of summer freedom, the merging of inside and outside spaces.

By the wooden bridge near her apartment, a large group of swans are resting on the habitation raft. As she crosses the bridge, they decide to strike out on the water, settling their white feathers as they go. She stops, leans over the rail, and watches them swim away downriver.

We must now take our leave of the Bo-Tree enclosure and push on to the wonderful city of Anuradhapura where we will rest for the evening. As we approach, open park-like scenery takes the place of dense forest, with an arrangement of ebony, satinwood, and fig trees. The climbing plants are no less striking with golden crowns of climbing lilies, mosses and a multitude of ferns. Large blossoms of champaca shine among glossy green leaves. Their flowers will fall soon, but they will come again when the rest of the plant is bare, always reviving, waiting to bloom. The air is quiet with a rich sweetness of jasmine and through the silence comes the sound of cicadas in the trees.

In the distance, the mountains, covered by thick forest, rise like dark waves, reaching up and up towards the sky.

Acknowledgements

Julia's story was initially inspired, in part, by Josceline Dimbleby's *A Profound Secret* (Doubleday, 2004).

In researching this book, the following sources were particularly useful: Reginald Farrer's *In Old Ceylon* (London Edward Arnold, 1908) and Leonard Woolf's *Growing: Seven Years in Ceylon 1904–1911* (Eland, 2015).

I would like to express my thanks to Cécile Lee and Clem Clement at Les Fugitives editions, and to Mary Flanagan and Anna South.

CHARLOTTE BEESTON was born in Cheshire and grew up in Kent. Further to a law degree at Exeter University, she worked as a solicitor for several years. In 2012 she obtained her Master's in creative writing from Birkbeck College, University of London, and won the Dissertation of the Year Prize. Her short stories have been published in the *Mechanics' Institute Review* and in *Untitled Books* online. She divides her time between London and Occitanie, in southern France, where she started writing *The White Flower* after the loss of her mother.